New Age Gothic

A Flame In The Night

Copyright © 2023 by Morgan Dante

Cover art by Andie Lugtu
Twitter: @siroc_co
Instagram: @levantwinds
Print store: https://www.inprnt.com/gallery/sirocco/

ISBN: 978-1-7331699-2-9

Content Warnings

Past sexual abuse
Past forced prostitution
Past abuse
Blood kink
Self-harm (for vampire bloodletting)

This is a romance novel for adults, and it involves several explicit sex scenes. If you don't like reading these, please be warned.

Chapter 1

Léon

As he reclines in the back of a smoke-hazy room the color and shape of a hexagonal sapphire, Léon Laflamme sighs over his black bottle of red port wine as his opium pipe gets low.

How *very* typical. With a cinch of his brow, he opts to ignore his crystal glass and swish his fingers around the neck of the bottle. The wine has a tart and sweet berry taste, and it further softens the room of dapper gentlemen in black, a murder of striped flat caps and vests. Even better, because opium, no matter its flowery fragrance, tastes bitter; the wine's flavor helps steel his tongue.

At the table closest to Léon's near the stage, the men with terrible headache-inducing cologne are speaking about backgammon. Oh *no*. Spare him. If only there were any lines in the club to snort his boredom away. How could these men live with inconveniencing Léon like this? He taps his fingers on the table as he waits for the burlesque performance.

Doldrum, doldrum, doldrum.

In Paris, no less! But even excess can become routine.

He should've brought the laudanum the physician prescribed him for his shell-shock. Through the din of chatter, he's numb-aware, a feeling he cannot describe to anyone in a way they'd understand. He feels the tremor of autos outside, which remind him trudging through muddy roads in the rain with his gun and bayonet slung atop his shoulder. The mustached man closest to him coughs and snorts wetly, delightfully, through his nose.

There's some consolation. For example, he's starting to float.

Another example: So far, Léon is the most stylish man here; yes, he's dressed like everyone else, but the black accentuates his long waves of blond hair, which tease the faux silk emerald-green tablecloth.

Or rather, his perfect locks accentuate everything he wears.

Though, there's a bloke he sees across the room, past the waitress with the sparkling plum-red cocktail dress. Oh, dear God, is that a crimson cravat? It's terribly archaic and yet intriguing, like garnet-red rose petals spilling down the stoic man's throat. It breaks through the farce of elegance. *See? War, what war? It's over. The dead are buried. Forget them. Watch our pretty dames take off their kits.* Though many of the gentlemen in the crowd have gold watches and buttons, all of the gold in the club is false.

Léon inhales another draught of dulce-sharp wine, his knuckles white. When he sets the bottle down, he places both hands on the table, rotating his bronze wedding band in that trench of skin that's turned pink with its presence. His eyes drift to the stage as, through the numb-awareness, a man announces the arrival of the seductive Claire La Cour. Anticipation laces his relief.

Claire, his darling. His second life.

Slow, tantalizing jazz burbles out of the speakers. When the lights brighten the stage, Claire emerges into existence, already curled languidly atop a stool, gazing at an oval standing mirror as her long legs greet the audience. The soft blue beams complement the short golden curls framing her heart-shaped face and her brazenly scarlet lips. Her skin is pale and smooth, her cheeks perfectly ruddy. Bouquets of iris and calla lilies wreath her head like a Bacchanalian halo.

Her attire is an enticing contradiction of nature and death. Her bodice is a deep midnight black with cobalt lace petaling it; even the laces are stunningly blue.

And at her hips spring bright red carnations, roses, and poppies, with the white lilies stark about the sea of crimped blood.

Léon finds himself forgetting to draw breath as she unspindles her body to arc her arms in ostentatious movements. She's a demure but deadly chthonic goddess who dishes out daisies and hemlock in equal measure, the frills spiraling her stem as verdant as her gaze. Here she is, death and the maiden, demanding that her ghosts rise.

Her green eyes glitter like the chandelier above, but as she casually unlaces her bodice, slowly revealing the plush of her breasts, her gaze cuts through the gloss and smoke and strikes his heart, which throbs in his throat. His mind spins like a wheel as its cold edges warm and soften.

She's not wearing her wedding ring; during performances, she never does.

A tug at his chest, and as Claire looks away, Léon finds his attention drifting to the gentleman with the red cravat pillowing out of his black suit. Léon feels as if he only saw pieces of the man, which now drift into the poppy-slurry of his pleasantly fractured mind. The man's profile is distinct with a prominent, pointed nose. His skin is wan in an almost sickly way, his profile reminding Léon of a bare skull, of depictions he's seen in museums of the gaunt King of the Dead. If the man ever had features, they had long ossified.

The stranger lifts his long, spidery fingers and sets a cigarette against his lips, which are red and plump as if he's wearing lipstick, or he's been kissed mad. As Léon drinks wine and watches, he shallowly inhales the smoke, not inhaling it for long before it plumes out of his barely parted mouth. Above his top lip is a wisp of a mustache—his hair is pale and cool. Silver.

Despite the color of those thick waves, not quite as long as Léon's luscious tresses, he doesn't look older than forty, despite his narrow face and the pronounced sickle line cutting above his high jutting cheekbone. He emanates both age and an austere beauty not easily claimed. Lavishly long hair not unfit for men of old, wiry, a decadent accent to his clothes, but a stern and confident demeanor settled to his thick, heavy brow.

Before Léon can pretend he isn't staring at a stranger, a man, as his wife performs burlesque and sheds her spare clothes—

As if feeling the look rolling against his face, the man meets Léon's eyes and impassively holds his stare with only the faint rise of one of those distinguished brows. Those lupine eyes are a steely gray, darker than his silver hair and rippling like mercury.

Léon, transfixed, grows taut when the space below his navel stirs. This is the most radiant man he's ever seen, and naturally, he's never used the word "radiant" for another man.

Swallowing thickly, Léon looks away.

No, he doesn't, even though he tells himself to. His jaw holds firm.

He looks away.

No, he's soaking in that man's gray stare, sharp but the color of rheumy waves during a storm.

They are the only two people in the world.

Léon curls his hands against the table, and they ache. His vision tunnels, and—

The room abrupts in applause. Léon startles, and the stranger simply looks back up at the stage and raises his broad yet thin hands to clap.

With uncharacteristic fumbling, Léon scrambles to the back of the club, which has none of the moody slips of light. Entering an open through, he lopes into a cramped rectangular room with six vanities. Claire sits in the middle left one and, in a satin floral pink robe with the elbows scuffed sheer, she converses to

Marianne, another performer with a corona of burnished auburn curls, draped, too, in a seafoam-colored robe.

Noticing him, Marianne grins coyly and rises to approach him. He sees himself in her watery blue eyes. Him, aloof.

"Hi, Léon," she says. "You're looking dapper today."

"Thank you." He offers a feline grin. "I could say the same to you." Naturally, I cannot stray from my goddess, but your performance was delectable as always."

"Oh, always the charmer. 'Goddess.' Most pals I know call their women 'baby' or 'babe.'"

"She's not my woman; if anything, I'm her man." If she hadn't approached him outside the Le Monocle, vaulting off her pale horse and grinning at him while she wore a black tux with a carnation that matched her eyes in the breast pocket, well, he wouldn't have had the couilles to approach her. Imagine, him, no couilles! He'd never had an issue wooing women—or men, when he was made to in the past or after the war when he was homeless and sore for francs. But it was true. Rather than making him bolder, alcohol and opium made a timid coward of him.

And Claire, well, she's Claire. She had been to war, too, but she never discussed driving an ambulance or needing to help discard swampy buckets of amputated body parts. All she spoke about was sharing her cot with some of the other drivers, all women.

Léon leans to give Marianne a butterfly-light kiss on the cheek. "Have a wonderful night, my dear."

Still sitting at her stool, Claire reaches out with both hands. "Marianne, Marianne, you *cannot* leave without giving me a kiss."

Marianne pivots on her heel and washes back to Claire, bending to embrace her. "Maybe I'll give you more than one."

Claire murmurs, "Please do." And Marianne does, pressing a kiss to each blossom-cheek before she departs the room.

When they're alone, Léon saunters over to Claire, and they wrap their arms around each other. He inhales the citrus tang of her shampoo, which mingles with her rosy perfume. He lowers his chin, and as she lowers his collar, her lips pepper their way from his throat to his chin to the corner of his mouth. He shifts and gently hovers his lips over hers, basking in the remaining buttery matte red smearing against his skin.

When he opens his mouth, her hot tongue laves against his bottom teeth, and Claire deepens the kiss, ruffling his hair with her exploring fingers. He tastes spiced wine on her lips as he surges into her ardent push.

After she pulls away, there's only a hair-length between them, and he nudges her forehead with his own, his rumpled hair like a ravaged curtain between them.

Léon says, "My dear, you were opalescent. Effervescent, even."

She runs her hands down his lapels. "But was I effulgent?"

"Obviously."

With a wry smile, Claire taps his closed lips. "Oh, stop. You're so very Léon tonight."

"I thought that was your favorite version of me. I could be Charles, the put-upon monk repressing my basest desires."

She threads her fingers through his hair. "You'd have to cut your hair."

Léon jerks away, a hand on his heart as he feigns grievous offense. "Oh, woman, your cruelty is boundless."

"Come," Claire murmurs huskily, rising with her hands on his waist, "let's go home." The space between her brows tenses. "Are you okay? You look a little unsettled." Only Claire can see through him like this.

At least, that's what he thought.

"Yes," he replies smoothly.

Without an ounce of self-consciousness, Claire sheds her robe and stands by her stool, fully nude. Léon plucks up a slash of black fabric and helps pull it over her head and tugs the sleeves, loose as water, over her arms. The dress, loose with an untied sash, falls down to her knees. Were they in America or England, she'd be positively scandalous.

As he takes both tails of the sash and fluidly ties them over her stomach, Léon asks Claire, "Are you hungry?"

"No, only tired."

"Now, now," Léon jokes, "you don't need to try to escape my cooking."

"Oh, beloved, you know I would never try to escape your divine tartines."

Léon sets her black satin bonnet, adorned with a fake black rose, atop her head and fiddles with the wide brim to get that perfect crookedness that makes Claire look both refined and wild.

"Of course," he says, cradling her jaw in his hands. "I know you too well. Besides, no one can reject my plum jam."

She molds her hand against his own and turns her head, kissing his palm. "I was thinking of the ones with garlic and chives."

In the dead of night, as phantoms of light convulse in tarantellas on the black water, they stumble along the Seine to their apartment over a barber shop. Rain stains dapple the off-white ceiling, and the sofa is missing an end cushion. The wallpaper is the color of a calcified peach. A chill hangs in the air; thank God he can turn on the furnace, now that the war's done and civilian use of coal isn't as strained.

In their bedroom, red light from the nearby hotel ribs the entire room and Claire's face as she slips into bed. She wears a pale yellow satin nightgown with sheer lace with designs of spiraling leaves around the low collar and sides. Sleeveless armholes whisper down to the top of her hip. He dresses in his night trousers.

As he lies down, and her body molds against his, her chin on his bare collarbone.

They don't make love because the opium makes him drowsy. Maybe tomorrow, when the world is less of a delightfully warm soup.

Léon wishes he could distill these moments in a liquor. Claire, poised and distant to everyone, except him. Even when she offers affection and dry humor to her friends like Marianne, she's wary.

Yet he feels there's a part of her that she keeps even from him, a secret locked box only for herself.

It's okay. He has his hidden boxes, too.

Chapter 2

Léon

As night slithers into his marrow, Léon sleeps deeply and dreams that he's phantoming through a cemetery by the sea. Fog scallops the edges of the nearby stone church in murky, arthritic fingers. He drifts by the stone wall, careful not to cross over any grave dirt.

His eyes focus on the shadow of the church, where it seems so dark it's like a rip in reality. The small hairs on the back of his neck rise. His heart roars with the waves far below the cliff.

The shadows convulse, and two red eyes flicker open.

Léon should be frightened, but he can't look away. In the war, he was almost on the precipice of death. Poisonous gas ripping apart his lungs and splitting his body open with furious red blisters that bled pus over trenches of mud, piss, and rot.

Instead, he thinks, *I faced that, so give me everything. I deserve it.* Surrounded by gilded decadence despite his paltry sums, and all Léon wants is for strong hands to grasp his shoulders as burning lips claim his. He wants to drink in kisses of equal smoky tenderness and teeth.

I could eat the world for what it's done to me.

The shadows embrace him, Léon's heart pounding hot and fast in his constricting throat. He needs it now: the touch; the burning; the softness, after.

Approaching the inky shadows, Léon's boots scrape against the swollen petals of poppies.

He'd ashen the entire world to have that.

I deserve more.

Léon surges his mouth toward blood-red lips as his hands dimple velvety swirls of shadow where a person's hair should be. He ghosts his hands down, and he's shocked to find he's trailing a feather-light touch over a chest with silver hairs and a collage of white scars, some raised cuts, some chasms.

He pushes, and his lips meet cool shadows.

He's kissing the moon, and it's colder than damp churchstones in winter. His chest aches, no, it burns, and Léon breaks the kiss to look down in horror as smoke sizzles between his collarbones, his silver crucifix falling into the blackening crater in his flesh.

Léon's eyes twitch open, as Claire's deep breaths plume a tattoo across the side of his neck. The ceiling above almost scorches white with the intrusive sunlight, tinged pink from the sign that never shuts off and always adds a hue even if the apartments are utterly dark. While sunny Claire appreciates the constant light, Léon wishes that some darkness belonged to them. When he would go between apartments and streets after the war, darkling corners were bastions of safety and peace because he could sit and collect his thoughts without fear of judgment or reprisal.

Regardless, as he watches the sunlight form a wide metronome on the ceiling, his attention drifts downward at a constant twinge under her trousers. It's no surprise to him; even if it can be inconvenient, it's natural for him to occasionally have a full mast when he wakes up.

With one hand, he vises his crucifix and swallows deeply. *God, save me from the trials and tribulations of a surprise maypole. Amen.*

Claire releases a soft sigh beside him, her body tensing with the dripping honey of wakefulness. He pities her, like he pities himself. Because why not? Self-pity is like indulging in dark chocolate on a rainy day. It's a shame to wake up from pleasant dreams.

He furrows through the groggy morning-clouds of his mind to remember his dream. Darkness. Graves. The sound of waves. A moonlit kiss, a light-dark embrace like fire and smoke.

Claire adjusts and looks up at him sleepily, her brilliant eyes shining like agates.

Léon presses a light kiss to her forehead. "I fear I didn't have anywhere near enough wine to have a morning headache."

She pouts in sympathy. "Poor thing."

"I know. How can I be a proper addict if I never have enough opium or wine?"

"You might as well be a teetotaler."

"Surely." His tongue is dry, and there's a tug in navel, in his stiff cock.

Claire's eyes soften. "What is it, beloved?" Her eyes drift to the sheets; she can't see his erection through the sheets, but she knows him well and gives a wry smile that crosses with a mock pout when she juts out her bottom lip. "Oh, dear. Are you having a morning problem?" Her voice is as light as last night's rain.

He grunts, cocking his head to the side on his pillow. "Yes, I'd say so."

She comes close and presses her hot mouth to his ear. "Do you want me to help you fix it?" Her breaths against his skin only make him release a strained moan.

Claire raises herself up to her knees, and Léon's attention cannot help but drift to the swell of her breasts under her rumpled nightgown. With ease, she uncovers his problem with a single toss of the sheets.

She hooks her fingers against his waistband, her knuckles small hills against his habit trail. Teasingly, she takes her time dragging his trousers down as he raises his ass in assistance and crooks an arm behind his head.

"Very helpful," she chimes, as she dips her hand farther and wraps her hand around the base of him. He sucks in a sharp breath as she starts to slowly stroke him, applying just the right amount of pressure.

Léon reaches up to cup her chin, and as he shifts awkwardly to rise, she closes the agonizing distance between their lips while still gripping him.

Too soon, she releases him. Despite years of experience when it comes to controlling his release, his arousal is pulsing and threatening to drive him mad. Claire pulls away.

"Please, love," Léon murmurs. "I want to please you, too."

Before she stretches out beside him, Claire pulls her nightgown over her head. Léon glances his fingers over the plush of her hip. She stifles a laugh when he glides his hand over her side, which tickles. He reaches her generous breasts with pink nipples, one of which pebbles under his circling thumb. She gasps as he presses his tongue to that sensitive part of her.

Like a sweep of bows in an orchestra, they move in tandem. Claire falls on her back as Léon goes to kneel between her legs. Léon admires her glossy waves of hair spilling on the pillow, and the darker blonde hair under her arms and at the crux of the sweetcream of her thighs, where he roves his fingers up the soft skin, faintly raised in some places with silver stretch marks.

When she was with her violent former companion, who doubled as her pimp, he forced her to keep thin. Even when Léon met her while she was free, the melancholy hollows of her eyes had been sunken in, and rarely did they have their magnificent color.

Now, she's bloomed.

Léon leans down to press a kiss to her inner thigh, and she releases a throaty laugh.

He raises his head and says sardonically, "I'm happy my lovemaking is funny. It's a new routine I'm trying out." He basks in how she looks at him from the pillow, her gaze half-lidded.

My Claire, my life, my pearl, mon coeur. So long as she's with him, he can brave the sea of life.

"I'm certain that'd make a good stage performance."

He makes sure that his breaths tease her swollen and sensitive clit. Already, she's starting to glisten. "For me, or for you?"

Bowing down, his tongue teases a lazy circle around her clit, and she gasps. Lightly setting his thumb there, he licks her there as the two fingers on his other hand press against her drenched entrance. He can't see it, but he imagines her toes curling like when she has sex with other people.

After a few more ministrations, she shudders, her hips thrusting upward. As her orgasm thunders in her, Léon holds her thighs and watches her cry out as he rises. She extends her arms and touches the top of his arms, sitting up to smash her lips against his, one of her teeth scraping his bottom lip. Blood mingles in their mouths as they seal them together, salty copper.

She combs her fingers through his long locks, and she softly guides him to the center of the bed, where he sits up with his legs spread and his burdensome arousal fully erect. She slips down and a jolt of pleasure spikes through him when her tongue slides across his tip.

Unbidden, Léon smells the sweetness-laced but prickly horseradish and garlic odor of mustard gas. Not because it's there in the room, but it hangs in his mind like cobwebs in a long abandoned house.

Léon's throat closes, and he chokes. His hand shoots up to his neck and digs into it. He starts to cough, and Claire has already stopped, sitting up with kiss-swollen lips and concerned eyes. Mouth contorting, she cups his jaw, never breaking her gaze from his.

Her voice is steady through his narrowing world. He feels too seen, too exposed. "You're here with me." Sweat, mud, scattering cacophony. "You're not there, beloved. You're not there. You're, you're here, and I'm here for you."

Léon sucks a breath through his nose and folds against her, his head on her collarbone as she settles her arms around him. "I'm sorry, I'm sorry."

Claire whispers against his hair. "It's okay."

It isn't.

I can't keep doing this to her.

If Léon says as much, Claire will tell him, no, he's not a burden; she understands. Certainly, they've had their nights where she's become so crippled with the past that he's had to help her dress and bathe, and she returns the favor.

His vision refocuses, and he reluctantly eases away from her, meeting her gaze blearily.

"Better?" Claire murmurs.

He looks down at his lap, his arousal already cinders. "I think it's stopped me in my tracks."

"It happens," she replies, caressing his shoulder. "I'll make some coffee."

At their small round dinner table in a room that smells of mildewed curtains, Léon sips on coffee as he wears an unbuttoned long sleeved white shirt and trousers, and so does Claire.

Léon's mind creases with the image of the man with the red cravat. He hasn't had a person strike his thoughts this much since Claire first approached him, while he was moony and half-drunk, at a club.

He should've approached the gentleman and asked for his name. He hates the feeling in his gut, that disappointment from a missed opportunity he can't truly characterize because he never tried at all. He's not supposed to be like that; the night's supposed to be his.

What for? To what end?

With the monstrous things you've done, you shouldn't inflict yourself on anyone else.

If Claire hadn't understood him unlike anyone else, he wouldn't have married her, and she wouldn't have married him. Neither of them need someone to make them forget; they need someone to empathize with when they remember. They already have their escapes: wine; opium; sex.

Hell, it's as if they were pulled together. For every moment they fought having someone else in their lives, they couldn't stay off each other.

Léon's hands fidget against a nick in the table. He really needs a smoke right now. "There was a man at your show."

Claire settles a cheek on her closed hand, elbow on the table. "Yes, I counted quite a few more than one."

"He had this very antiquated cravat. Completely out-of-fashion. I saw him, and he completely and utterly compelled me."

Her brows raise in interest. "Really?"

Léon stares into the dark ripple of his coffee. "When he met my eyes, it was a shocking feeling. I don't know how to explain it." That's a partial lie, even to himself. He felt that way when he first saw Claire, but it's not necessarily only curiosity or desire or love. Rather, it's a secret fourth thing.

"We should find him. I always love meeting enticing strangers."

Her idea sparks a flame in him. A purpose, as silly as it is to think, *Ah, finally, I know what to do with my life: Find the stranger I stared at rudely at La Orquídea Violeta while my wife was undressing.*

That thought takes root in him. *Claire was on stage, but I only had eyes for him.* It wasn't a lack of desire for Claire, but rather this burgeoning curiosity that disturbed him. Yes, out of all the feelings he listed, curiosity is the closest one. These alternate possibilities, were he to eat the fruit.

I'm not attracted to men. It's only business.

Léon states, "I wouldn't know where to start. I couldn't tell if he was a tourist or not. His clothing certainly looked outdated."

Maybe it's the eyebrows. Like the man, Claire has thick brows that only augment her smoldering gaze. Maybe his admiration of nice eyebrows transcends man or woman.

After they fall into a companionable silence, Claire tells him, "I have a job at Natalie's manor tonight."

That perks Léon up, his intrigue only equal to his apprehension. "I'm assuming it's not a job reading *My Ántonia*."

Claire pushes back feathers of her hair. "If only sex could be that erotic."

"Will it be filmed?"

"Yes, a stag film." No black-and-white film can ever fully capture how radiant she is. "Will you come with me?"

He remembers her old words to him, two years ago:

I need you with me in case something goes wrong, or an actor or director gets violent. I need someone on my side.

Léon reaches across the small surface and rubs the top of her arm. "Always."

"Thank you."

"How long of a night do you think it'll be?"

"I'm not sure. I suppose it depends on what trouble we can find." Claire sighs. "I hope it's with other women and not a man."

Léon grins. "Are men other than me really that terrible in bed?"

"Oh, stag film directors can have such a limited imagination. It's already seen as radical to have a woman nude and not being blank-eyed as still as a plank as she wears a hitched up nightgown and waits for her husband to finish. Most directors don't want anything except the most ordinary missionary imaginable. It's as if we're in America."

Léon replies, "In America, you can't even film that without a prison sentence."

"True enough."

"For your sake, I hope it's profane enough to be banned by the Pope."

"I wonder if I'll get to fondle myself with a vacuum cleaner attachment again."

Despite his fumble early in the morning, his arousal starts to stir again.

She says, "I could handle a woman, or a man, or many women and men, but I don't think I can abide by a vacuum cleaner."

"And why is that? I imagine its suctioning ability far surpasses mine."

"I'd say you're both equal. It was only a little strange, that's all."

"Good, I've always hoped to have as much proficiency as these newer machines."

Claire drapes her fingers over his. "They aren't so new anymore, but you, darling, are always fresh. What did I do to deserve you?"

Her words startle him, so much that he almost recoils. Because she sounds so very much like *him*, and he's the one who's supposed to think that.

"Funny," he mutters, bringing her elegant hand to his lips. "I often ask the same thing."

Chapter 3

Claire

The opium-laced air of the manor sways as figures lounge on plush red chairs. The gold console tables hold crystal opened bottles of cognac and absinthe.

While her husband is dressed in a simple black suit with a stark white shirt, Claire wears a sleeveless, sequined red dress that ends in tassels halfway down her thigh; she has no undergarments. Similarly, tassels mane the low V-neck.

She hadn't spent long with her makeup and attire; there's no need to fixate on what will be smeared and removed, and besides, the films tend to prefer a truly demure, unmarked look. In their dingy, plain wooden wardrobe, most of their clothes are concealed in plastic. At the bottom of the wardrobe there are scattered black rice-pellets. Mouse droppings.

Without words, as they pass halls of ottomans and sofas where people, men with women, women with women, men with men, neck and grind against each other in various stages of undress, Claire motion her head to Léon. He winds his arm around hers.

The oozy, thriving music plays so hard from the radios and speakers that the manor, draped in opium smoke and poppy-red wallpaper, and pearled chandeliers, trembles. In some passing rooms, films are playing to rapt audiences.

Often, the watchers are men, staring and sweating and rising as they cross their legs to conceal their tents.

She's never understood how men who went to burlesque clubs and stag parties, where they'd watch erotic films in the same small room together, missed the blatant homoeroticism of getting hard together as a bonding activity

When they find the scene room with swirling floral red and sapphire-blue wallpaper, they're greeted by a vast king-sized bed with silken crimson covers. Besides the man behind the camera, there are three women, two with far longer and darker hair than her, kissing and fondling on the bed. Beneath the creamy slash of their sheer and rumpled night, she can see the darkness of hair at their pubic bones.

Claire's chest grows taut in anticipation, as Léon moves to sit in the corner. She likes that he's here because, as selfish as it is, he's the right mirror.

When she looks into that reflection he's made of her, she sees a desirable and capable woman who's smart, confident, and beautiful. She had the same relationships with Lauren and Anna and Marge in the war.

But there were also times people showed her a vapid and shallow waif to be used and disposed of. A handkerchief. A punching bag.

She can't imagine any of those debilitating perceptions have ever crossed Léon's mind. And to reciprocate, she shows him a humorous and compassionate man, the sort of person who will make a good father one day. It isn't despite their mistakes that they're worthy of each other, but with them, too, in mind.

One day, once they are steady on their feet.

Electricity crackles and tightens the air, sprouting thick with musk and perfume as she rolls her dress over her head. Already, her nipples are hardening as she's beckoned to join the smiling pile of long legs and expert fingers. If Claire had been born in a fantastical life, she'd probably be a nymph in a bright meadow full of wanton fellow nymphs and well-endowed satyrs.

She feels Léon's eyes sizzling into the small of her back when she approaches the bed. At war, she could handle herself, and she likes to think if put in danger by a bold director, she'd be able to fight back. Nonetheless, Léon's presence makes her feel less on guard. She isn't self-conscious about her nudeness being filmed; but she's had directors get fresh and try to corner her.

When she kisses a woman with brunette hair and honey-eyes, the other woman's laugh is as sweet and bubbly as sherry wine.

Claire laves her tongue against the woman's wet mouth as her scene partner's hand roams to cup her breast. Claire is sure to kiss each of them as they undress out of everything but their stockings.

They all rest on their sides and form a loose circle, or perhaps more like a square. One of the other women, nymph with freckled shoulders, gives a long lick to her clit while Claire stares between another woman's thighs, She adjusts her back and shoulders in what's a complicated but not unfamiliar position. Pressing two of her fingers against the honey-eyed woman's sopping entrance, Claire dips her tongue into the wet pink folds.

Chapter 4

Léon

After the filming is done, Claire has dressed and slipped the francs in her purse. She and Léon sit on a sofa in the hallway with cushions as smooth as water. Claire leans back against the plush and shuts her eyes for a moment. Her hair is damp from a shower in one of the many available washrooms, the ones not inhabited by lustful guests. Strolling through the hall and strewn along occupied sofas are murders of crows and peacocks, dazzling knee-high dresses and sequined suits of black and robin egg blue and turquoise, with feathered, askew masks.

Claire's eyelids flutter open, and Léon takes her hand in his as she stares at the ceiling and murmurs, "This is enough for this month's rent, but I think I need to find more work."

Léon lifts that hand to her shoulder and kisses her cheek. "Let me try to do something. You look tired."

She smiles at him and nuzzles his nose with hers. "I'm not too tired yet. Let's see what's been prepared to eat." All day, she's barely eaten, which would worry him if he didn't know she was merely unsure what trouble they would get into with what orifices, so on days they went out to party, she kept her meals light in case some daring chap wanted to do a little Venus aversa, as the Romans would say.

"Besides opium and absinthe?"

A frown. "My dear, if either of us have those on an empty stomach, we may not get off the floor."

Léon gives a playful sigh as they stand. "Fair enough."

The immense dining room is a paradise of fake lilies and corpulent chocolate-covered strawberries, beside, of course, an array of wines and spirits on a table that could easily seat a hundred people. Léon relishes the sweetness of the desserts, especially when they cross from dulce to tart and mild. The entire room is a Dionysian delight.

As Claire sits in a chair with a velvet cushion and nibbles on a strawberry her eyes scan the room until they fall in the corner. Sitting beside her, Léon follows her attention, and his jaw clenches. His own eyes can't help but widen as he sees the guest not partaking in any food or drink.

It can't be, but it's deniable. That glance of long waves of silver hair until his gaze fully settles on the man who takes too-brief puffs of a cigarette, as if pantomiming the bad habit for appearance's sake.

"That's him," Léon whispers.

Claire looks between the stranger and him. "Really?"

"Yes."

She blinks, and then she makes a noise of approval. "Ooh, you have good taste in men."

He says coyly, "Better than you? Be honest."

She gives a dainty shrug. "Who says that I can't find you both irresistibly handsome?"

"You could," Léon relents. "But what should we do now?"

"We?"

"I suppose I like to try to get group feedback."

She urges, "Go on, then. Speak to him. Engage."

"Are you sure?"

Claire grins wickedly. "I do believe I was the one to suggest that you try to find him."

"That you did. I didn't expect it to be so soon. What will you do?"

"I'll be okay. I know how to handle myself among fellow hedonists."

Léon doesn't doubt it. If anything, he's wary of how he'll feel without her by his side. "All right."

He stands and approaches the man, who's conspicuously inconspicuous, yet again with that damned cravat and his position in a chair at the dark corner of the room, the nearby hearth creating a streaky chiaroscuro over his already distinct, sober countenance. Léon can now truly appreciate how healthy and lusciously thick the man's curling hair is, despite its unusual color. It almost looks as if the man were born with silver hair, rather than it going gray. Then again, premature graying happens. It's only a hunch.

The man's flinty gray eyes only meet Léon's once he's very close. When he stops, he suddenly feels stupid and aimless. He looks back at Claire, who gives him a reassuring smile.

Léon looks back at the man, who regards him inscrutably. "Greetings, Monsieur."

The man barely moves his head to look at Léon. "Hello." He takes another pitiful drag of his cigarette, expelling it as soon as it enters his mouth.

Léon squares his shoulders as his eyelids flutter in partial offense. "You don't remember me?" It can't be so. He knows to the world, where he's a disposable whore, he can be a drunk and an addict and a louse. But not forgettable. That idea is insulting beyond measure, ever since he was born as a fourth son in a row of five other blond brothers. But none of them had ever pulled off anything with finesse like him. Léon had never let being the son of a hostler deny him refined tastes.

"Yes," the man says in his deep timbre, like the most sumptuous bourbon that also has that scorching tang. "You were at the club."

"You made quite an impression."

"I would hope so. I would be bemused if I didn't, with how long you stared at me."

That's not fair. Now he's making Léon feel a little bad for his faux pas.

"My apologies, Monsieur. It was never my intention to be rude. All I was doing was admiring that cravat. I don't think I see many people with your fashion." Yes, the man's black suit is very long, something that might be usual on the street...in the

1850s. Not that Léon would know for sure. That was long, long before he was a gleam in his parents' eyes, with the gleam being their tears once they realized they'd have another mouth to feed.

Léon doesn't see the man fluidly stand, but he does, his suit rustling, and he realizes that the man is about half a foot taller than him, well over six feet. "As it so happens, I was going to venture into one of the viewing rooms. I'm enticed by these moving pictures. I remember a time when there weren't any."

The first motion picture was made in 1888, with the first true film being in 1902. They were fairly common now, but he supposes that perhaps the man never sought to catch any. Many don't, seeing such a nascent medium as crude and a waste of time. A fad.

"Certainly," Léon says, "I'd be happy to watch one and talk over wine."

"Oh," the man replies, "I don't partake in alcohol." Nevertheless, he follows Léon.

That's how Léon finds himself in a room full of other men seated around tables as a projection plays of one man fellating another. Despite the ever-present sweet perfume lingering like clouds, the air smells of booze, acerbic cologne, and perspiration. The silver-haired stranger next to him, though, smells both smoky and metallic. It's not an unpleasant fragrance.

The circumstance surprises Léon. Not the stag film, but the fact that it's two men. Of all the illicit films he's seen, most are between a man and a woman, while some are between women. The films are only five minutes long; the previous one that played featured three women bending with their buttocks facing the camera as a fully dressed man came and, his back to the camera, took turns vigorously rocking against them. In many films, no one even bothers to take off their oxfords. Others wear black masks.

Léon's expression is blank; little can surprise him about sex, but he appreciates the bluntness of *Soldiers' Greeting.* He pretends he doesn't notice the charge in the room; after all, while many stag parties feature men who'd never, ever dream of sleeping with another man, this particular manor encourages different tastes. And it's that mission that leads to him conversing with the stranger he saw at a burlesque club as, in the background, a rake of a man leans over on a sofa as another spreads his legs, displaying the thick black juncture of hair trailing toward his half-erect cock while his partner takes it into his eager mouth.

"Do you mind if I ask for a smoke?" Léon asks as the man giving pleasure strokes the other man's balls. The silver-haired stranger obliges and gives Léon a cigarette and a clunky brass lighter, his own old one crushed in the ashtray in the center of the table, settled in the back of the room near the door.

"Thank you," Léon says, deeply inhaling the acrid smoke as the man takes the lighter back and lights a new one. "So, what do you do for a living?"

"I'm a chemist. An alchemist, to be more precise. I study both physical and metaphysical properties."

"Ah. What's your name?"

The man stares ahead, the shadows looking at home on his lupine face. "Matthias."

"That's lovely."

"I've been called many things. By allies. By enemies. 'Lovely' is a new one."

"My name is Léon."

"Hm. I see. What's your profession, Léon?"

"Botching job interviews. I'm a bit of an adept. No one can quite remain as hopeless as me."

"What does she mean to you, the dancer?" Matthias glances at his wedding band. "I saw you two arrive together."

"She's my wife. Claire."

"Really?"

"Yes. Did you think I was having an affair? What an unforgivably naughty thought. We are a good Christian couple. As such, we copulate only on the first Tuesday of the month in the missionary position, as God and Christ intended."

"You must trust her, to allow her to have that profession."

"She's my wife, my companion, not a trophy."

"Yes, of course, that disposition creates less jealousy."

A rebellious lurch in Léon's stomach. He's made a mistake. With his secrets, with Claire's, he can't trust this man. How could a wanderer of Paris' midnight gloss understand war, desperation, and death? He'll use them as fucktoys and discard them once he's sated his curiosity and loneliness.

Léon doesn't mine being fucked, especially for money; he just wants to make sure he's not fucked over. And he won't tolerate hurting Claire.

Watching the short drag Matthias makes of his cigarette, Léon says with a hint of humor, "You must barely taste the tobacco."

"It's a reflexive habit, nothing more. I don't even taste it."

"Ah. How are you enjoying the film?" Léon asks jovially, elbow on the table. While he leans against the table, Matthias is ramrod straight in his chair, regarding the lurid film more like a science project than an obscenity.

"It's pedestrian," Matthias replies, "but it serves its purpose."

Léon can't help but agree; Claire's right when she labels most stag films as very reserved, even if they involve more than one person or queer sex. There's almost a sense of self-consciousness. In many countries, even swashbuckling America, the films themselves are illegal, and even where they aren't, the directors are aware of their audience and the limits of debauchery. In a paradoxical time of sexual freedom and restriction, taking it in the back is seen as an illusive fantasy.

So, it's nearly explosive when, in the film, one of the men props himself up, crossing his arms on the armrest and thrusting his ass in the air as his partner moves behind him and, inch by inch, slowly slips in his cock.

Around them, other men begin to breathe deeply, and he's fairly sure up front he sees someone ducking their head in another man's lap.

Léon watches their faces contort, but when he looks covertly at Matthias, the man doesn't.

"I suppose," Léon says, inhaling smoke and letting it settle in him before expelling it. "I'm afraid I'm not a true homosexual."

"I'm not sure what that means. A true homosexual, as opposed to a false one."

"Not without payment."

Matthias arches one of his broad brows. "And then you're homosexual?"

"For an hour, or less. Probably less."

"I can't tell if you're humoring me."

"I am being dead serious."

"But you still love your wife."

Ardently, Léon replies with a puffed out chest, "Of course."

"Hm, both men or women. I think there's a word for that."

"When I don't have a pecuniary incentive, any arousal I have near men vanishes." Léon feels a dangerous urge to challenge this man. To scandalize him. "Have you ever been with a man?"

"Once, yes. In my previous life, I had three wives, a mistress, and a fellow veteran I tussled with."

Now, that's fascinating. "All at once?"

"No, polygamy isn't legal."

"That's never stopped anyone."

"It was over the span of many years." That's good. Léon likes talking to people with several experiences; a man who's had various marriages will have interesting stories.

At least, in theory. In truth, Matthias is so self-serious and reserved that Léon can't imagine him bearing his soul, his heart, or his cock for anyone.

That's an enticing thought, isn't it? A challenge. A peek through the mask. Not the many masks surrounding them, but Matthias' impenetrable stone face.

What lies behind it? Maybe it's dark.

Even better.

Léon hopes to find out.

Chapter 5

Claire

When Léon leaves with the gentleman, Claire waits at the dining table, having long lost her appetite for the delectable strawberries and raspberries.

Thankfully, in a party as eventful and cacophonic as this, she doesn't need to wait long before she encounters someone interesting. Or someones, rather.

Firstly, an imperiously tall woman in a top hat comes by and gives a green rose to every woman at the table. When she looks at Claire, she offers a sly smile, her long brown hair flowing out of the hat. Claire has always admired people with curly hair that bounces like it's alive, regardless if it's yellow like Léon's or dark as a countryside night.

"Merci," Claire tells her before she goes, kissing the woman's cheek when she briefly arches down.

Across the table, she catches the dark blue eyes of a stranger with near-black hair spooled on his shoulder, his shoulders square and broad. From what she can see of his face behind his horned ivory mask, he's a looker.

A tension stirs in her navel. He wasn't staring at her before, but the moment his eyes fall on her, they hold that smoldering gaze.

Another reason Claire prefers women when filming scenes is that she doesn't need to worry about preventing pregnancy, as unlikely as it might be with her long periods and cramps that hint at a disorder that affects her ability to conceive. She's only ever had one abortion. Right now, like a lot of women she knows, she has a small metal ring inside her, and she hopes it's enough; it's worked so far.

Flashing a grin at the man, she asks, "Enjoying yourself?"

He meets her expression in kind. "Yes, quite, with a view like this."

She languidly pushes her cheek against her curled fist, setting her elbow on the fine, lacy tablecloth. "Have you come with anyone?"

To her surprise, he pulls off his mask, revealing a face as unlined as hers. "No. Admittedly, I'm new to this scene. It might not have been wise to have come alone, but I don't quite have anyone I'd reasonably ask to come here. May I ask your name?"

She pauses, before saying, "Claire."

"Claire. I'm Henri."

Like mercury, Claire slides out of her chair and comes around the table to the man, exaggerating the swish of her hips. When Henri scrapes his chair back at an angle, his eyes burning with need, she waits for his ghost of a nod before she sits in his lap hip-first. He wraps his arm around her waist.

Lowly, she tells him, "I'm here with my husband."

"Even better. I wouldn't dream of leaving anyone out. That is, unless he'd be opposed."

"I'll have to speak with him. I don't mean this to judge you, but that's unusual to want him there. I don't think I've ever heard a man say he wants another man around."

She likes it, someone who surprises and entices her. Most men interested in women at these festivities are fine having sex near each other or watching stag films in a full room, but they don't want to touch someone like them.

Then again, while she knows it's rare, she knows men who prefer both men and women, or simply don't care.

"It may be unusual, but that's why I'm here. I don't come to a party like this to be bland. I have enough of that at my job."

"Would you care to sojourn elsewhere? I don't want to take too long and worry my husband."

Her words are honest—yes, she doesn't want to disappear completely on Léon—but she can't help but remind a stranger, even one who is enthusiastic about another man's presence, that, yes, she has someone here who will look for her in case any trouble happens. Just in case.

She isn't bluffing. Even at this stage, when everything feels easy and natural, she can never be too careful. She hates that she must invoke her husband, as if what she wants or doesn't want isn't enough, but often, it isn't.

After she untangles herself from him, Claire and Henri are fortunate to find her husband and the fascinating silver-haired stranger outside one of the viewing rooms outside the dining room. When Léon sees her, his eyes soften and then flicker to Henri, and back at her.

He sweeps an arm to the side. Ever the one for theatrics; it's what makes him fun company. "Love, this is Matthias."

Claire extends a hand to Matthias, and she's delighted when an agile grip takes hers and kisses one of her knuckles. His touch sends delicious lightning up her arm, and tension ripples in her chest. "A pleasure to meet you, Monsieur."

He releases her hand. "No, Madame. The pleasure is mine."

Léon says flatly, "I didn't get a kiss."

"Oh," Claire steps forward and flutters her lips lightly on his mouth.

Léon

The next moment, the four of them find an empty scarlet room with a king-sized bed draped with silken sheets and a canopy festooning the entire mahogany frame. Matthias, predictably, stands by the door, though the gesture is less awkward and more like he's blending into the gold and red rose wallpaper.

Truly a different kind of wallflower.

Meanwhile, as Léon stands with his silver-haired acquaintance, Claire and her new nightly beau are kissing by the bed, one shoulder of her dress askew.

The room smells of smoke and incense and sharp cologne, though the fire below the mantel is low; this room pops with lips smacking against one another and the crackle of flames.

With the stoic mask he's kept on the entire time Léon's spoken to him, which, in fairness, has been thirty minutes at most, Matthias says dryly, "I imagine I should go."

Léon starts, "Yes, I think that would be—"

Her hands on the new man's chest, Claire breaks the kiss and calls out to them, "No, don't dismiss him."

Léon swerves his attention to her, and her eyes radiate with pleasure in having surprised him.

She tells him, "I want him to watch."

Chapter 6

Claire

When she glides over to Léon, he gently takes Claire's hand and asks her, "Are you really sure you want him here?"

Her eyelids flutter as she gives a little smile. "Yes, if you want it, too."

He gives a little laugh. "I knew you'd put it like that."

She strokes the side of his face. "I want to make sure you're okay with it." It's the truth. Though they're both rather bold people, she never wants him to feel as if he must do something to please her.

"I am, in theory. This isn't like anything we've done before." Usually, the other partner is a woman. "And I, I haven't been performing as I once have."

"For me, that's thrilling, the promise of something new. How do you feel?"

The sharp prickle of arousal stirs in his groin. "Yes, I agree." He looks over at Matthias, who regards them distantly. "Will you stay?"

Matthias gestures his hand up, pinching an unlit cigarette. "May I smoke?"

Claire and Léon exchange a look. At his ghost of a nod, she says, "Yes, of course." She's not entirely sure why he smokes; from what she's seen of him in the hall, he barely inhales it, mostly lets it burn.

With both hands on his, Claire guides her husband close to the bed, where Henri waits patiently. Carefully, she toes out of her pumps.

When both the men stand side by side, she places a kiss on both of their lips before kneeling on the soft carpet and beginning to unbutton Henri's trousers, as Léon undoes his.

Practiced, she frees Henri's cock, and he sucks in a breath when she uses unscented oil from her purse on her palm and starts to stroke him from base to tip.

When Léon has released himself, Claire takes her free hand and does the same for him, the space between her legs pulsing with her heartbeat and slick arousal. Léon leans down to brush her hair behind her ear. Despite his quips, he can really be quite sweet.

Then, she lightly applies her tongue to the ruddy, leaking tip of Henri's cock. As she tastes his salty come, his breaths grow more labored as she gives a few short licks, her mouth forming a small O as she prepares to take him in her mouth. Her dress suddenly feels constricting. The fabric's friction against her breasts is pebbling her nipples into hard peaks. A string of her sticky arousal slips down her thighs.

She continues to rub her husband's length, circling her thumb over his slit, as she applies more pressure to Henri's tip, glancing the ring of her lips over the skin before, inch by inch, wetly swallowing him until her lips touch where her fist is wrapped around his base. As the heat of the room makes the crook of her arms damp, her nerves come alive as the debauchery of it all, all too conscious that she's being watched intensely by a third man in the room. Despite the bed being partially in the way, when Claire briefly stops and leans back, she can see him on the ottoman by the closed door, one leg casually slung over the others, his smoldering eyes as piercing as a hawk's, before she begins sucking off Henri again.

Then, with a smack and pop, she removes her mouth from Henri's glistening cock and turns her attention to Léon's. With expert ease, she engulfs him as she pleasures the other man with her oiled hand. He swells and stiffens more in her mouth, his arousal now a dripping mix of saliva and pre-come.

When she rises, Léon pulls her into a passionate kiss, his tongue laving against her own as she grabs at his ass and he presses a hand flat to her chest, the edge of his thumb teasing where her hard nipple temples out of her dress. His silver crucifix is cold against her skin.

Another hand, Henri's, tugs at the thin, sequined black fabric on her shoulder, and she lets them both help her pull off her dress until all that remains are her dark stockings. As she tugs off their own clothes. Her pulse beats fast in her throat and between her ears like a frantic bird.

Then, all three of them are on the bed, Henri lying on the pillows as she crawls on all fours between his legs, flattening her tongue and offering a playful, long lick to his balls before trailing a line up his entire length as she feels Léon settling on his knees behind her.

She expects Léon to enter her immediately, but he doesn't, ever the considerate lover; maybe she only wanted him to because her need is reaching unbearable levels. The only reason she didn't finger herself to completion was for this moment, so she can ride her climax with her beloved inside her.

Léon rubs his fingers lightly over her clit and dips his touch down, easing two long fingers into her dripping wet lips. She moans around Henri's cock, having to work to keep herself from shaking in pleasure and a need to go further. As delectable as it would be to be taken roughly, she enjoys her husband's patience.

He then starts licking her, and she gushes around his ministrations.

With a delectable idea in her mind, Claire raises her head to see Henri's arousal-darkened, hooded gaze fixated on her. He wraps her hands above her hips as she goes to straddle him and teases the tip of him with her dripping sex, roving her hips and crying out when his cock brushes against her tender clit. She shivers in pleasure as Léon massages his artful fingers from between her shoulders to the small of her back, supporting her as she lowers herself on Henri, and he fills her.

She ruts atop Henri, hands on the light down on his chest as both men keep her steady, and when Léon reaches around to fondle her clit, his hair hanging like moss and tickling the skin of her shoulder, her visions goes flame-white as she peaks, her first shuddering climax long and sweet as she drives Henri deeper and deeper into her—*God, oh God, oh God*—until the fullness almost aches. Léon continues to circle her clit as she rides out the remaining beats of her pleasure, ready to be refilled again.

"Lick me," she whispers to Léon as his chin grazes her shoulder blade, and he burrows a kiss into the side of her neck, trailing it to her nape. When she feels his beautiful silken hair, it's times like these when she most loves that he has longer hair than her.

After a pause, Léon shifts to the side of both her and Henri, as he leans between them, over where they messily join. Electricity throbs between them all as Léon throws his curtain of hair over his shoulder and bends to lap at her clit.

Already, Claire feels her pleasure mounting again. As her mind slants and grows greedy for more extreme heights, she only wishes they were both inside her, that the man watching them would join them as the center of her mingles with the fluids of all three of them.

She gasps then as, in their quickening pace, Henri's arousal falls out of her, and without her needing to request it aloud, Léon grips the other man's cock and helps guide it back inside her. The mere gesture brings her close to another fluttering release as she and Henri resume, but not for long before, reluctantly, Henri slips out of her, leaving a sticky mess between them.

Henri raises himself and breathing raggedly, presses a hot kiss to her ear. "Baby, I want us both inside you."

Chapter 7

Léon

The idea makes her pause, even if it's as if he read her mind, and she's enticed. She climbs off him, poised on the center of the bed, so achingly close to another climax and a mix of desire and frustration. And, more than ever, that insistent need to go further and further. In her past work, with her pustule of an ex-lover, if he could be called such, he'd made her do many deeds for francs, so there's little that she hasn't tried, but she wants to reframe those traumas into joys. To prove that no one can take control from her.

Claire looks at Léon, and he shivers with how vulnerable he feels. "Léon, can you prepare me?"

He nods at her. "Yes."

As Henri braces himself on the pillows, also looking on the edge, Claire moves to face Léon near the side of the bed, where he's gone to retrieve the oil. Her body flushes when he gingerly spreads her legs farther by touching her knees and easing between them with a bottle in one hand.

She moans lowly when he licks the outside of her rim before plunging his tongue into her ass, and then adding an oiled finger. When his tongue leaves, he sets in another finger, gently stretching her as her nerves sing. Despite her instincts, she tenses and shudders as he tips his tongue into the entrance where her skin and his fingers meet.

"Yes, yes." She pants heavily. When he's done with her, and she's ready, she says, "Léon, I want *you* to do it from behind."

A contemplative frown. "I'm afraid I'll hurt you."

Claire balances herself with both elbows. "If you don't want to do it, that's okay, but I trust you more than anyone. I know if you did that you'd stop." Her only requirement for a position like this is that she must be upright; if she were lying on the sheets, she'd feel less in control of the rhythm.

When she gets up and turns, she rejoins Henri, and he assists her in letting him enter her again. A hot wave spreads through her when Léon settles behind her, and two sets of hands settle on her. She hitches a breath when he sinks the first of him into her lubed hole.

Oh, God. Oh, fuck.

Léon releases a suppressed groan as his tip presses its way into her tightness. Claire deals with the struggle of letting go while dealing with the intensity of all the sensations. She gasps at the heightened pressure of two men inside her, the overwhelming clash of touches and musk and cologne and smoke. Henri stops as they wait for Léon to adjust.

As her husband continues to ease himself into her, and she's all too aware of the friction of two swollen cocks touching and rubbing between her perineum, and Matthias staring at them all, her heart pounds hard in her chest as her throat tightens.

She's so close, basking in the utter decadence of it all, even if she can feel Léon holding back. She's not sure why. If he's afraid to hurt her, or if he's afraid that he might lose his arousal because of the opium; it's all easier with cocaine, but she doesn't like when their minds are muddled either with the sluggishness of too much of the pipe or the frenzied drive of white lines of powder on the table.

Then, the men start to move clumsily, out and then deeper into her, slowly going until they find an easy, sinfully slow pace to thrust into her. Sweat trickles down her temple as she pushes down on Henri and rotates her hip, and another orgasm, more blinding than the last, crashes into her senses. Her body floods with heat and nerves, jellying her limbs. It takes all her strength not to fall on Henri's broad chest.

Léon reaches over her shoulder and laces his fingers with hers as his body molds against her back, and waves of warmth roll over all of them, so much that it makes her deliriously giddy.

With his deepest thrust, Henri cries out, and she rides him and draws out his release. He twitches inside her as she feels a trickle of heat as, collapsing from the exertion, he rests in her, softening.

To Léon, Claire murmurs, "Baby, beloved, come here." He should know what she wants; he knows she likes what comes next.

He slowly slips out of her, careful not to hurt her as she shakily climbs off Henri and, with her husband's help, lies on her back beside the spent man. With a devilish grin tight on her lips, she motions for Léon to come close as she wraps her hand around his base and gives a few efficient, if crudely swift, jerks until his seed bursts out of him.

He paints her offered chest and throat in heaving spurts, coating them in hot pearly lines as her breasts fall and rise.

A few minutes later, in the washroom, she wipes herself with a cloth as Léon cleans himself. Claire must always be careful not to get an infection from improper or incomplete aftercare. She takes some time to sit on the rim of a tub the size of their entire apartment washroom, and she collects herself.

What comes after is a haze of near-dissipated passionate tension, but not quite. Matthias still sits by the door, one leg lazily over the other, not saying a word to any of them. His presence only further electrifies the burning room, Claire's exhaustion stymied by a stirring pulse between her legs as, still naked, she sits by the glass coffee table by the fire, where the powdery residue of cocaine still lingers from whatever festivities came before their revelry.

Léon goes to sit on the edge of the bed, still getting his bearings, and Henri sweeps beside her, and she pulls him into a wild kiss, her arms looped over his broad shoulders, which ripple under her touch. She can barely make room to breathe with how she inhales his scent and taste. The pressure in her groin soon becomes a tightness in her chest, waiting to be unraveled again.

Reeling for another go, Claire guides Henri to the scarlet poppy rug beneath them, and rolls on her stomach, rising to her hands and knees and offering herself to him. And then, Léon is there beside them, and on the floor, she lets Léon rest on his back and settle under her, his breaths pluming across her lower belly as Henri lubricates himself and presses one experimental inch into her ass. She releases a low moan as her husband nudges his nose against her pubis until he goes lower to stroke his tongue over her clit. His arousal rises under her, and she wraps him in her hand and pumps his length as Henri pushes deeper and opens her up to the brink of pleasure, where the faint discomfort isn't painful but rather gives the sensation of utter fullness. Completeness.

Her eyes going upward as the rhythm heightens, her attention flickers to Matthias, and she brazenly holds his gaze. As the rug fibers scrape against her knees and palms, her heart jumps.

She's shocked at how composed he is; given the scenario, she doesn't think it's that poor form to look around his lower region, and she sees no sign of arousal. His composure only augments her rapidly growing need because even in the frenzy of sensations, she can't help but wonder what it'd take to unspool a man like Matthias.

Nevertheless, their momentum isn't as relentless as it was on the bed; even so, it doesn't take long until Léon's mouth shudders against her soaking core and he goes stiff, spurts of climax splashing in erratic arcs on her chest. His last clumsy licks sends her into a spiral that renders her mind black, as Henri's breath hitches, and he slips out of her, and she feels wet heat sputter onto the small of her back. They all collapse in a messy tangle on the silk rug, the room a stark inferno with the writhing hearth. Though she rests on her side as Léon caresses the hair from her face, caged by two bodies as spent as she is, Claire can't help but raise herself on her arm and look toward the front of the room.

Matthias is gone. Not even a goodbye, but then again, how does one make casual conversation with strangers after what just transpired? She still can't help but huff and wonder if the enigmatic man is forever lost to them.

That is, until she notices a white dash of something on the seat, a folded note where he was sitting. At least, it seems so.

Curiosity spikes in her, and Léon's gaze follows hers.

Chapter 8
Léon

The next late morning, as Léon stares at the ceiling and rain patters the window, his contentment soon fades into another emotion.

Doubt.

How did it come to this? How did everything escalate?

Matthias, so reserved, and yet content to watch the most decadent sex.

More perplexing still, Léon had another dream of the cemetery and the red eyes, and a kiss that consumed him.

Last night, Matthias penned his address on a creased piece of paper.

So we can talk in private.

And a command: *Come at night.*

Come at night. In private.

Not even vaguely suspicious. And Léon can't help but have even more doubt creep in.

He tries to lighten up. After all, last night was incredible. Sometimes both the alcohol and the opium make him too lethargic to even consider sex. Last night was a reminder of *Oh right, I can still fuck. Good. Had me worried there.* He thanks his little guy for actually showing up. He hasn't been this refreshingly tired after a session since Claire used a harness and exhaustively reamed him.

When Claire stirs and opens her eyes to meet his, Léon plants a kiss on her brow. She nuzzles her face into his collarbone, and he remembers a distinct feeling he tried to cast away last night.

And as Claire gazes at him with that shrewdness sharp and refined in those green eyes, he knows that she knows his choice. Only one other person has looked at him like that, with a stare that says that they know him, perhaps better than he knows himself.

There's something else. When Claire had her mouth on him, Léon had the urge to kiss the other man, and the thought had almost sent him over the edge right then, and he would've felt guilty for messing all over Claire's dress.

And Matthias, well.

Should he really even bother to find him? As alluring as the thought is, how enticingly perilous, what do you say to the man who watched you have sex with your wife with another man?

He and Claire had already discussed this before they drifted into a satisfying sleep.

If you want to go to him, then go.

"Do you want to come with me?" Léon mutters to her, his hand rubbing her back through her nightgown.

"Hm. Not tonight. I think I need to rest. Unless, unless you'd be more comfortable with me there. I certainly would like to return the favor."

He frowns. He wonders if they'll ever reach a stage where they don't feel like they owe each other, as if they've granted each other a transactional kindness simply by keeping each other company.

More cynically, he wonders if, in the end, this is all relationships are, and all they can be; for all her optimism, Claire might even say as much: Life is about clawing your way to having the best, no matter how the world tells you that you deserve nothing. You're owed nothing, the world will say, as it expects everything.

And Léon likes to think, well, maybe they *are* owed something.

At least, they should approach life and demand health and riches. God makes all these promises and tells those who love him to pray when they need Him, and he showers his chosen ones with gifts. Is Léon really meant to accept that life is job rejections and trauma and failure with the occasional promise of sex, wine, and opium as a relief? Because that's how life is.

If the world is their own making, he says that life should give them more, then why shouldn't it be so?

He's not a fool. He knows that their way of life isn't sustainable long-term.

Léon kisses her forehead. "No favors necessary."

As the sun slinks down in the pink horizon, the taxi fumes tumble away from an estate that's bigger than Léon would've guessed, with a wrought iron gate that's been left open, creaking with the leftover wind from the earlier storm.

Matthias doesn't live in a house; he lives in a stone mansion with sharp, slate-gray, uneven turrets. In some ways, it reminds Léon of a gothic castle, even boasting gargoyles around the lip of the roof.

With a deep inhale, he sets his hand on the swinging gate, stopping it. The metal is wet and cold.

The cobblestone paths, amid red rosebushes and forlorn trees weeping their golden leaves, are winding, branching out into different smaller paths, but converging toward a wide set of stone stairs. They lead up to a high mahogany door, framed in black iron, that doesn't look like it'd be out of place at the entrance of a parish. Léon raises a palm and touches the wood, thinking of how many knocks to slam against it, and he's surprised when the door groans backwards, opening up to a hall lit by a brazier.

He's already seen so much. Survived so much.

Unto the breach once more.

With one graceful step, Léon invites himself in.

Chapter 9

Léon

Palming his crucifix, Léon steps on a white and black checkered floor ringed by vermillion carpeted stairs that spiral upwards. The main hall is massive and lined with sofas and gilded chairs the same color as the carpet. On each side of Léon, high square archways are framed with latticed iron that twines like vines. At the bottom lip of the stairs, a brazier blazes, and candelabras straight out of a penny dreadful rise out of the floral black and gold wallpaper, between gold-framed oil paintings with vague figures he can't make out from near the front door, which he carefully, quietly shuts.

He takes it all in, black jacket slung over his right shoulder, and his nostrils burn when he breathes in the dust and hint of mildew.

"Hello."

Léon jumps and sets a hand on his rabbiting chest, just below his silver crucifix. "Christ."

To the right, where he sees a glass cupboard with rows of porcelain plates, Matthias steps out of a slice of shadow and into the dimly lit hall. His hair is loose and as curly as Léon's.

Léon jokes to himself, *I wonder if he has any ears under there.*

He's dressed in a burgundy coat over a white shirt with a ruffled collar and cuffs, which is untied at the neck, revealing a triangle of skin and pale chest hair. His trousers are a deep gray. No cravat like rose petals this time. A shame, as Léon imagines grabbing it—what is happening to him?

"Not quite," Matthias replies, drawling a rasp of breath from a cigarette. Léon can't help but roll his eyes. The light and darkness play harshly on his distinguished features. Near him stands an imperious grandfather clock with its face like the moon, or a single golden eye. "I'm surprised you came so soon." He doesn't sound surprised in the least. "Do you require anything?"

Léon squints, the flames not enough for him to see much past the coronas they cast on the wall and floor. "Light."

"Ah. Yes. There's a switch by you."

Léon turns to find a brass plate of, well, not switches, but three little white buttons on the wall. He presses the one closest to him, and two conch-shaped lights framing the front door buzz on. He does the second, and a similar light blazes on at the cap of the lowest stair post.

"Hm. How long have you had this estate?" Léon asks. "Out of pure curiosity."

"A while," Matthias says, taking a few steps forward, so he's close to the center of the room, under a chandelier that glitters and lightly sways with an incoming breeze from the open windows like a crib mobile of crystallized tears. "but I don't always stay here."

Léon lolls his head. "Here? Paris, or this mansion?"

Matthias gestures loosely around the room with his cigarette, creating a lazy circle of smoke. "Both."

With the lights on, the room is cast in an infernal, beige-yellow light that only makes the dark parts muddy, but he can see better the three-foot blue and white vases around the furniture. However, whereas usually they'd be full of various plants, they're empty.

Léon's eyes flicker to the light at the stairs. Already, a moth thrashes its suicide tarantella against the bulb. When his attention strays back to Matthias, Léon is surprised at how the man's gotten so close without him noticing, as if he flashed from one location to another. He reaches out to the gilded console table by the door and rubs out his cigarette in a globe-shaped ashtray with gold and red rose designs.

"You barely used it," Léon says lightly. "Tsk. What a waste." He tries to shrug off the incessant knowledge that they're less than two feet apart, that the last time they saw one another...

Matthias straightens, shifting to look at Léon, except it's as if he looks past him. "The cigarettes don't do anything for me. It's more expected for someone to smoke around others. It's common, an accepted tic. I simply become the man smoking in the corner, rather than just standing around."

Léon scoffs. "Don't tell me you dress like an eighteenth century baron, sans the flamboyant powdered wig, because you want to blend into the shadows."

For the first time, Matthias smiles. It's reserved, but there. And very sharp and white, almost wolfish. "That's a fair point. Perhaps even without thinking about it, I've been sending signals."

"Your house is quite spectacular. At least, the few square feet I've seen have already surpassed my lofty expectations. Do you live alone?" A covert—well, not covert, but a more polite way of asking, *Do you have a wife? A companion?* It isn't so uncommon for affluent men, transients seeking out the grandest highs they can find, to have torrid affairs, sometimes with other men, while having a wife. Léon has never much understood it. Claire is his partner, and he'd be remiss to step out on her.

Yet here you are, without her.

But she does *know that I'm here.*

Matthias inches close, eyes half-lidded. "Yes."

Suddenly very warm, Léon saunters near the steps and rakes a finger across a console table below a painting of nymphs in the rivers like water lilies. His touch creates its own river with a bank of dust. His back is to Matthias. "No maids or live-in butlers?"

"No," Matthias replies, his voice both distant and close. "I don't remember what it's like to live with someone."

Léon picks up a ceramic green dragon, rotating it and looking from the red mouth to pebbly scales to the intricately crafted wings. "All those marriages and lovers, and you don't remember?"

"It feels like centuries ago, and the longer it becomes, the more alien the idea of starting again is."

Léon sets down the figure. "You could fit quite the long line of consorts in this place."

Matthias' voice comes shockingly close. "Is that what you would do?"

Léon swivels around and finds himself leaning his back against the table, his hands reaching behind to grip its edge as Matthias regards him from about a foot away, his cologne smelling of roses and ashes and something metallic but indiscernible. "It's what my wife and I would do." He's all too aware now at how Matthias is taller than him, and his stomach flutters.

Matthias tilts his head. "You two do everything together."

Léon swallows thickly, his collar sweltering. "Yes."

"She isn't here now."

Flagrantly, Léon inquires, "Do you want her to be? I saw how you looked at her, when everyone except you was inside her."

Matthias leans forward his gaze smoldering in his otherwise stone face. "It wasn't only her I was looking at." Léon must control his breathing to keep himself from breaking, from—he's not sure what he wants to do. "I suppose looking at others, seeing them see me, is the only true way I see my reflection."

"Really?" Léon replies flatly, one brow raised. "I don't think I've ever thought about it that way before."

"Well." Matthias steps back, giving Léon some breathing room. "Since you've come, feel free to look around."

"This isn't some ploy to lead me to a secluded room, is it?"

Dark mirth dances in those damnable gray eyes. "Oh, every room here is secluded."

Despite his best instincts, the same ones that tell him to put down the pipe and the bottle, Léon decided to take up Matthias on his offer. After all, if he must live the life he does, he won't pass up the opportunity to bask in decadence he'll never possess in anything but spirit. If it's a crime for his life to be anything, it's boring. He might crave some security every now and again, but he could never be idle.

Loping past the furiously spasmodic moth, Léon ascends the steps, eyeing paintings of classic Greek myth scenes between the candelabras: Echo at the well; Daphne half-changed into a tree, her mouth agape in terror or ecstasy as her naked midriff spirals into thick roots; Persephone eating the dripping, swollen pomegranate, the garnet juices trickling down her throat.

And then, a scene of ships with a blazing meteor with wings.

Never regret thy fall, / O Icarus of the fearless flight / For the greatest tragedy of them all / Is never to feel the burning light.

The entire mansion is a clash of old and new, much like Matthias. Though there are candelabras, there's also electricity Matthias turns on as they go. Léon marvels at the first washroom he comes across.

The tub, sink, and commode are a pristine white, the mirror untarnished from foundation powder and chalky toothpaste. An iron radiator waits under the curtained window, but what intrigues Léon the most is the linen closet, and another regular closet—regular! It's the size of a bedroom—with clothes hangers that boast silken robes with curling blue, green, and red designs of lilies, roses, and of course, poppies.

Matthias remains at the washroom door, barely passing the threshold. Léon steps back and looks into the mirror, hoping to see the other man's eyes, but the doorway doesn't appear in it. Unsatisfied he goes back to looking at the clothes, eager to paw at them.

"Do you ever wear any of these?" Léon asks.

"No, never. They were left over from the previous owners. They aren't quite my style."

Léon grins mischievously and looks behind himself. "I know I would look magnificent in these. Wouldn't you like to see me in one?" He almost doesn't believe the words that pour out of his mouth, prompting him to think, *What do I want here, exactly?*

Matthias rolls his shoulders. "If you want them, they're yours."

Léon pouts. Oh, Matthias and his brooding inability to answer questions. "I can't afford even a scrap of them."

That inscrutable stare the color of a winter storm. "I didn't ask for payment."

He cannot help but feel tired and sad at how vast this space is, and yet Matthias feels detached from it all.

Dryly, Léon says, "Not in francs, perhaps."

Matthias waves a hand. "The money doesn't matter to me."

"Oh," Léon replies, sure to give a dramatically long sigh, "how I wish I could feel that way."

"Yes." Matthias grips the dark gray door frame. "It certainly is a privilege I've garnered, regardless of whether it came easily or with difficulty." He looks out into the hall. "Come."

Léon replies dryly, "You don't need to ask me twice."

"I can show you the garden. It's lovely at night."

Léon will admit: He doesn't care for plants. They don't make for interesting conversation. Yes, he does like his opium, which comes from a plant, and he can admit that many excellent meals and parts of life come from plants. Indeed, humanity would be doomed without them. Still, well, they just exist.

All that aside, Matthias' midnight garden is beautiful, with that ephemeral quality of nature just before a hard freeze. a blanket of mist shrouds the grounds, and Léon cannot help but feel like he's in a dream.

The cemetery.

In the center of the winding, white stone paths is a circular fountain, set between two lion topiaries and scalloped with rose bushes growing wilder than he's ever seen one twist in the city, the bright scarlet flowers, at the final stage of their bloom, are only thwarted by their thorns, looping and pointed as barbed wire.

All the rest of the garden, with its sage, chrysanthemums, and late-blooming, spotted, pink stargazer lilies, is fashioned into rows of square arrangements of red, red-pink, and yellow.

Instead of a simple wood shed, a stone building with an angular roof stands in the back right corner of the land, its walls ribbed by layers of flowering moss. To Léon's surprise, there's a greenhouse in the back left corner.

"That's one of the passages down to the cellar," Matthias explains, standing by Léon's side.

"Ah. Don't take this the wrong way, but I wouldn't have taken you for a fan of gardening," Léon replies.

"It isn't as if we had plentiful conversations when we first interacted."

"Fair enough."

Fireflies swing in the air, mirroring the winking of some of the stars in the inky night sky. Léon sticks his hands in his coat and leisurely sways as he walks back toward the fountain, admiring how the water strikes silver—like Matthias' hair—in the moonlight.

Matthias joins him and sits on the edge of the grooved stone fountain, which has fleurs-de-lis grimaced into the surface. "What do you truthfully feel when you see all of this?"

After some deliberation, Léon sits beside Matthias, so they're only a hands-length apart, and answers, "As opposed to how I dishonestly feel?"

"You could lie."

"But let me guess, you could tell." When Léon looks behind them at the back of the mansion, he's met by the sneers of not only gargoyles, but these figures he can't quite recognize that look vaguely like wolves, except that their limbs are far too long.

"There are tells, but they're different for everyone."

"I feel lightheaded thinking about what I'd do with all those closets and cupboards. Imagine, I could own thirty very similar blue shirts and place them in a closet and barely fill it." Léon mulls over his next words. "It's beautiful, but very empty. I'm not sure I'd want to live here alone. I get mad when I have no one to talk to. The decadence does help, but after enough loneliness, I might have to start an argument with the wallpaper to survive."

Matthias looks up, and the moon strikes his gray eyes, and Léon is submerged in fog and sea and sepulcher. "What if I told you I feel numb when I look at all this?"

"I would say that to some degree, it's understandable. It's a lot to take in. Sometimes, we feel numb when we feel too much. It's a paradox, like how a leg going to sleep hurts. At the same time, you don't know what you have. Houses can be inhabited."

Matthias cuts his eyes away from the moon and stares intensely at Léon. "Do you think I'm ignorant? That I can't see what's in front of me?"

Léon tries to keep himself as nonchalant as possible. "To have such fine things is a rarity, a privilege, which you've already recognized. If emptiness or loneliness are problems, they can be remedied easier than gaining money overnight. Although, I have a more pressing concern that's yet to be addressed."

"And what is that?"

"Is your hair dyed?" Léon inquires.

When Matthias stares, Léon must keep himself from laughing.

"Last night, we watched a stag film together, and then I watched you, your wife, and another man sleep together, and you're wondering about my hair."

Léon flips his hair over his shoulder. "Well, yes, I hope the question was obvious. I even forewent the flowery language. No need to be so dramatic about it."

Matthias replies flatly, "I know that you are averse to drama. It's as blatant as your chastity."

"Of course, I'm practically a monk. Besides, I thought it was quite a good question, one which begs to be answered."

"No, this is my natural hair. I've never dyed it. Have you ever dyed yours?"

Léon leans back and sets a hand on his chest. "Please, how dare you. Why would I ever deny anyone the immaculate nature of my tresses? I forbid the very thought."

"Tresses," Matthias replies with an arched brow.

"Why, yes." When he relaxes, Léon adds, "That's good about your hair. It'd be a horrible pain to maintain that color, however nice it may be. Not everyone can be born with stunning golden locks."

"Are you talking about yourself or your wife?" Something about the question feels barbed, but Léon can't tell why. He wonders, with a dark delight, if Matthias is jealous of Claire. As mischievous as that makes him feel, and as much as Léon likes for his partners to be a little rough and domineering in bed, he can only handle so much possessiveness. After all, all his life, he's been a possession. Of brothel owners, of the military. A tool to be wielded and discarded as needed.

Besides, Matthias isn't his partner.

"Both. Were you born with it like that? Your hair."

"I wasn't."

"Then, what color was it originally?"

"It was deep red. Auburn."

"You were a redhead," Léon states. His eyes rake down the fall of silver, trying to imagine Matthias as he must've looked before.

"You sound in awe." A hint of sardonicism.

"Where are you from?" Léon asks, having rarely seen somebody with red hair in Paris. Not impossible or unseen, mind, but exceptional.

"Hungary. Győr, a city halfway between Vienna and Budapest." The way he says the last word, with an intonation both deep and like a hiss, is almost reverent. *Bu-da-pesht.*

Léon didn't expect that Matthias is from Hungary, a place he knows nothing about, but on further analysis, it makes sense. For the most part, the man's baritone voice is very careful with every word, and his accent is practiced. It only comes through when he says places in his homeland, as if his mother tongue provokes a homesickness that strips away his practiced removal of where he came from.

"I must admit my ignorance of Hungary." For some reason, he imagines crumbling castles and cold, bleak mountains. "Though I'm sure it's beautiful. Do many Hungarians have red hair?"

"No. At least, not when I was there. I haven't been back in a long time. And indeed, it was beautiful, especially in autumn. My hair, well, it ran in both my families."

Léon has to brace himself because he's not used to nor did he expect this casual conversation. Besides his talks with Claire, he's unused to finding out more about someone without an ulterior motive. You loosen a man's tongue, so he'll loosen his drawstrings. Arithmetic, if Léon was good at math.

Léon floats his hand, gesturing to Matthias' general, well, hair-area. "Why did your hair turn this color?"

"Age will do that." Léon clings to that wryness, that mere fraction of vulnerability and personality.

Léon presses, "You aren't that old." He might not have a right to demand such answers from Matthias inside his own house, but hell, if he asked most of anyone, they'd say with his past, he doesn't deserve to be alive.

Boldness seizing his heart, the seaside graveyard dream fogging his mind, his self-preservation, he asks, "May I touch your hair?" There's no un-odd way of asking, but he does ensure that he asks. Growing up, he was all too aware of what it was like to have no autonomy, for all the adults around him to say, *I will touch your hair or pat your cheek or squeeze your arm whenever I feel like it. Because you are a child, and children are helpless, and children must respect adults, no matter what they do to them. You have no say, ever.*

Matthias says, hands spread on his lap, "When you've endured certain things, you age, no matter how long you've been on Earth. If anything, for what I've been through, I look young. War, managing an estate. For years, I lived in Wallachia as a Count. Not far from home, but very different. A restless wolf under all masters. Always on the verge of rebellion and dissolution. The Habsburgs couldn't claim it because of the Russians and the Ottomans."

"The Ottomans have no claim to it now. Their empire is no more." After the abolition of the caliphate in March of this year, a military officer converted it into a republic.

Matthias nods pensively, looking away into the rows of flowers. "I've been a terrible host. I haven't offered you any tea."

"Yes, you have," Léon jabs. "I'm parched."

"What do you like?"

"I tend to prefer mint. Do you have any?"

"Yes," Matthias says. A pause. "Would you like to come inside?"

"No, I think I'd like to stay out here."

"A moment, then." Matthias leaves him, and Léon contemplates what to do next, what his true purpose is as he watches the glowing fireflies, blinking like pale eyes in the deepening night.

When Matthias returns with a steaming porcelain cup on a plate, the smooth white surfaces dappled with disarmingly soft pink roses, Léon asks as his host sits down, "None for you?"

"No," Matthias replies with a dismissive wave. "I don't drink tea. I merely keep it out of courtesy for anyone who does."

The mint aroma tingles Léon's nose and mouth pleasantly, but he hesitates as he looks down at the greenish-brown tea, lit by one of the hanging lanterns. It has nothing to do with the smell or potential taste.

"I thought you were parched," Matthias says, and then, just as casually, he adds, "If I wanted you dead, I wouldn't use poison."

Léon raises the tea close to his lips. "Your methods of seduction are absolutely stunning." After another wait, he takes a sip, not detecting anything off. Setting the tea down, he asks Matthias, "Were you in the Great War, too? On the side of Austria-Hungary?"

"No, not that one. Another one, years ago. Now, even when the world erupts in war, it passes me by. Wars end. No matter how long they are, no matter how many die. Empires fall, no matter their strength. The Ottoman Empire lasted for six-hundred years. Ancient Rome, for a thousand."

"Perhaps longevity is how long people remember. How long the effects last. I doubt anyone forgets how the Romans and Ottomans have shaped the world, even if there are no more Caesars or Ottoman sultans."

"It's hard, coming home from war. I often feel like I'm speaking another language as everyone else. That when I look at the sky or a river or a building, I see the world differently. Claire must've seen horrors at war, too, sawing off gangrenous limbs, but neither of us ever speak about it. What's there to say? I'm a soft creature made to lie on pillows, but I survived."

"And Claire?"

"What about her?"

"Is she a soft creature made to lie on pillows?"

Léon laughs. "If that were the life she could have forever, she'd happily take someone to bed every night. But soft? No."

"Do you two want a different life than what you have?"

"Perhaps." Léon isn't a fool, but he feels like acting like one. It can be refreshing to act stupidly bold. "I imagine a residence this immense has a wine cellar, perhaps an underground canal you use to remove bodies, or a tunnel that leads to the labyrinthe catacombs below the city."

"Yes, it does."

Léon stands, his arms swinging languidly at his sides. "Show me the cellar."

Chapter 10

Léon

When he gets to the bottom of the stairs, Léon gapes. Matthias stands in front of him, back facing him, since Léon thought that if he's doing this horribly reckless action with an enigmatic near-stranger, it would be best not to have his own back to his host.

When Léon imagined a wine cellar, he pictured a stuffy, dark location with walls of wine. What he didn't expect was the bowed ceiling, revealing that the little shed was only a path to a great underground expanse. This massive tunnel, with its rows of red stone pillars and casks, could very well be used as a mausoleum for a prestigious family.

Léon whistles.

"The bottles are on the wall," Matthias says, and indeed, there are hundreds of dark red wines on shelves. As Léon looks back at the other man, inspecting his hunched shoulders, Matthias looks a tad—awkward?

Awkward. Huh.

The cold removal is slowly being scrubbed away, leaving a man who's slowly revealing more of his life and himself.

A man who, despite his knowledge and demeanor, might be out of his depth.

"This certainly is a nice, clandestine place to get drunk in," Léon says, fully facing Matthias. "As far as places to get drunk at go. Not that I'm an expert."

"It's no den of pleasure." Matthias doesn't quite make eye contact, his eyes on Léon's face but seeming to look past him.

Cheekily, he replies, "Any place can be a den of pleasure if one is creative or adventurous enough." Léon hums. "You're a Count, you said."

Matthias crosses his arms over himself, angling away from Léon to appear as if he's inspecting one of the massive barrels. "I suppose that's one title I've had. It has a certain elegance."

"It makes me think of a gothic novel."

Matthias leans his head back, visible eye half-lidded in thought. "Yes, I don't shun that perception. There's an allure to darkness."

"Allure. You could have anything you want, but you watch." Léon can only imagine what would've happened if Matthias joined them last night.

Matthias goes very still, and Léon wonders, strangely, whether he's imagined the man breathing. "I haven't been touched by a lover in a very long time."

Léon finds himself mirroring Matthias, though he doesn't stop facing the man's profile as he crosses his arms, too. "It sounds like many things haven't happened to you in a very long time. Besides war."

"I've never considered having someone close, until…"

Léon cocks a crooked grin and demurely twirls a finger in his hair. "It's okay. no need to be modest about my enticing personality and impeccable hair on my behalf. I have that effect on others."

Matthias' voice becomes more distant, more like air. The damnable man still won't turn his head to look at Léon. "No, I'm not sure we are close. We barely know one another."

"And yet," Léon pushes, "you used the word 'until.'"

"I'm afraid it's difficult to say how I feel." Only then does Matthias face Léon, his countenance ringed with shadows. "I see myself as a spectator to humanity now, a ghost. I first felt this when I was at war."

Léon sobers. "I've felt like that, too. Like I'm disconnected with the war. Even when I partake, it's different. I can't relate to anyone who's never suffered and indulges in those parties. When I try to talk to them, it's as if we live on separate planets. I came home, and I'm not sure if the city was different, or I was. Everyone was freer, and so was I, but there's something else, an invisible lock."

That sealed box of secrets and grief and pain.

Matthias nods. "You put it well." He uncrosses his arms and drops his hands to his sides. "I also cannot help but feel the grief should be over by now, and the nightmares."

Grief.

His companions.

Léon asks, "Did you ever have any children?"

"Three sons, four daughters."

"Where are they now?"

"They're all dead."

Léon's heart plummets. He thinks of all he's been through, and despite all that, despite feeling as if his grief has reached deep and wide, to depths he never even thought possible, he doesn't know what to say.

"May I ask what happened?"

Matthias mutters fondly, "You would be the one to ask."

"I understand if you'd rather not—"

"Fever, for the most part. Illness. Many of them had meager health at the start, and time did the rest."

"I'm sorry. I can't imagine."

"I've been isolated for so long that I'm unsure how to accept condolences. Thank you, I suppose. Do you and your wife want children?"

Léon swallows. "Maybe. One day. We're focused on the present now."

It feels discourteous to have Matthias reveal a thorny piece of his past while remaining coy.

Léon works to find his words as he speaks. "Neither Claire nor I had much when we were born. We've had to struggle for what little we have now." He doesn't intend it as a barb at first, but it comes out that way. It's not so much that Léon begrudges Matthias his wealth, although disdaining exorbitant class differences might be the noble thing to do.

No, Léon enjoys fine clothes and food and wine. He likes sitting to the side of an orgy as he inhales opium out of a pipe; he likes watching Claire be with other people, and he likes joining in. Hell, she looks good doing it, and so does he. Léon could live his entire life in an opulent fuck-palace. In fact, that's what he was made to do. God only failed to grant him the funds to match his exquisite taste.

"Your wife is a dancer."

"Yes, and I'm currently searching for work."

"Paris is thriving. I'm sure you'll find something." Is Matthias encouraging him? It's odd that they're talking like this at all.

"She was a whore, and I was, too. Before the war, anyway. We worry about our pasts catching up with us."

He clams up, having said too much. Having divulged a truth that might've been all right if he hadn't brought Claire into it.

"How so?"

Léon can smell the smoke of that night, the itch of his delirious laugh.

I'm free.

He'd been delusional.

Matthias gestures forward, and they go around the casks to view a high honeycomb wall of wines. "You don't need to tell me anything. Léon, I know we don't know each other well. But I do want to listen. I don't know if I can help, or if you want help, so I won't offer that, but I'll listen. I can't say why. All this time, I haven't connected with anyone. Hm. Perhaps I've explained it to myself."

Léon is taken aback, especially over what Matthias says about standing back, like he does, and listening. He'd expected even a hint of his past earning either revulsion or pity, and the latter would provoke offers of "help."

"I was sixteen. They made me wear rouge and lipstick because that's what attracted the clients. You know, I look very good in red. Would you believe that I look smashing in a dress? That I like them? Especially the ones with sea colors. I just didn't like having no choice. I don't care if it makes me less of a man. I don't need to wear trousers and smoke cigars to know I'm a man."

"You left that life."

Léon abruptly laughs; he can't help it. "Left" is technically correct. "There was a war by the time I was nineteen. I went from one terrible situation to another, the next one having far more gangrenous feet and death, and fewer orgasms. When I was afforded them."

He's not sure he was ever allowed to be a child. He was always scavenging for his sickly mother, slipping his hand into pockets and memorizing alleyways for escape.

"Forgive my presumptions, but I don't think recruiters search for their best soldiers—"

"By scouting out young whores in the most fashionable dresses?"

"I wouldn't put it like that."

Léon says icily, "The truth."

Matthias holds out both his hands. "If you're looking for me to denounce you, it won't happen. There are far worse things than soliciting sex for money. Far worse things."

"Yes, on the surface. But for all you know, in the early 1910s I briefly went to the Americas and fought in the Mexican Revolution." That part is true, the first time he ran away from a brothel and stowed away on a ship.

It's true that Léon looks like the last person to fight, and fight well, but he'd grown impassioned by the arguments against the imperialist upper class, and his grandmother, Angelique María Martínez Santos, had been mestiza, with a mother and grandmother who spoke Nahuatl.

He served no major role in the conflict and, after the revolution's victory, returned to France to drink and whore himself in 1917, when he was found by his considerate owners and beaten; he's not sure why he didn't stay in Mexico City after the revolution. Maybe it was what he saw the Spanish do to Ambrose Bierce and swore to take to his grave. Poor Ambrose.

Or maybe it was because Léon felt a sick obligation to his home, an impulse that perilously mingled with self-destruction. As inexplicable as it was, he felt guilty when he left the brothel, where he'd received shelter and meals and was forced to whore, but when he thought it was force, he was ashamed because the two men who owned the establishment would argue, well, what, were they supposed to house an orphan for *free*?

And yet, as much as he disdained the Spanish upper class and its oppression of the mestizos, he can't help but want pearls and vintage wine and dresses and orgies all night in a glittering mansion where he can party all night and then doze with Claire in their own bed without needing to walk three miles on fatigue-wobbled legs. He doesn't want to conquer anything; he just likes the thought of being able to please himself and rest in one constant space.

Matthias shakes his head. "That's impressive, for sure. I don't think I understand when it comes to my own tastes. I've never felt a compulsion to wear dresses, but I don't see anything inherently wrong with it. You and your wife had these jobs."

"They were separate places. We didn't meet until later."

"And how did you come out of it?"

"Did we? You've seen what we like to do, and Claire does work in those stag films."

"Perhaps there isn't a stark difference, and they might be under the same category, but there is a variation between starring in illicit films and going to parties for a romp and what you once did. By the sound of your voice, one is more enjoyable than the other."

Any of those scenarios, regardless of if they're work or play, can be enjoyable, but it's the lack of sovereignty he had at the start that bred trauma and resentment. And a darker urge.

He blurts, "We both killed our pimps. I can't speak for Claire, but if I found a troubled soldier who had a similar story to me, hell, I'd fuck me, too."

Shut up. You're not only damning yourself, you fool. Think of Claire.

Léon anticipates horror. Instead, Matthias nods, this infuriating man, as if he *expected* a murder admission.

Léon's brow pinches. "Aren't you a little worried that we've killed people?"

And when those words leave his mouth, he realizes it's been over a year since his last nightmare about fire. Maybe it's the opium, or maybe it's his conscience letting go. He's not sure if that's good or bad. Guilt is burdensome, but it's a compass for how far he's lost himself. He's grown up with shame; what will he do without it?

He hopes for absolution, someone to say, *God still loves you. He forgives you. I forgive you, and I love you even if you are disgusting and sinful and ruined.*

"I've killed people," Matthias rumbles. "All that matters is that they deserved it."

Christ.

But is he wrong?

Matthias continues, as Léon realizes he must be gawking like a fool, "I know you are good, despite everything."

Léon snorts. "I'd love to see your evidence."

"I saw how you looked at her. It's rare to have devotion like that, especially..."

"Especially when I don't seem like the sort? I know. But how could I not be loyal to her? Claire is so much. Before, my life was in limbo, gray and lifeless, and then she burst into it, always strong and optimistic."

"Do you want her, truly, as a companion forever?" Matthias inquires. At first, the question seems odd, but Léon supposes many husbands would feign their affection for posterity.

"Of course I do. More than anyone. She's my heart."

"Do you want her singularly?"

"Despite what my past might have you believe, I'm not interested in men. In the past, I only endured what I needed, what others demanded of me, to survive."

"What if you could express any desires you have without fear?

"I'm not sure what has given you the impression that I'm restrained."

Matthias hums. "There's some sort of shame in you, perhaps its mere existence perpetuates more shame, like an ouroboros sustaining itself by devouring its own tail."

"Ashamed of being ashamed," Léon replies dryly. "You should be a poet."

"One need not be poetic to tell the truth."

Léon raises his brows. "Is it the truth?"

"We can go around asking circular questions—again, the serpent eating its tail. But only answers will lead to anything."

"Anything?"

A weary sigh. "Here we go again. What if you could escape the poverty, the rigmarole?"

Léon sobers. He wonders dryly if Matthias would give him the money to run away with Claire if he asked. Perhaps, but he realizes that not even he wants to test Matthias' altruism. Let Matthias claim him. *And what would Claire want?* "I would give anything for us to have a better life."

"Anything?"

Léon steps forward, voice lowering to a husk. "I'm not sure if I would give anything to you, but I could try. If I had anything truly useful to give. We could start. I could give you what you want right now, if you're willing to give me money for it." He comes up to Matthias and sets his hands against the man's chest.

Matthias grips his hands and shoves them away. Such a tease! "No, you couldn't. Believe it or not, That's not what I want. I don't want you to force yourself to be intimate with me if you truly feel like it's something you don't want."

"Really? You gave me a different impression last night."

"I did enjoy that, but that's not solely what I want."

"Solely," Léon echoes.

"I've lived through much, and practically, it's been best for me to live alone, but I'm not asking for your company in exchange for help, favors for favors."

"I'm not sure I understand." That's the world. Everyone wants something, and they rarely give gifts without expecting repayment.

"If you stay with me, you'll be safe. I don't expect you to do anything with me. Be anything."

"Then, why? What's in it for you? The mere joy of a good deed? of assisting charity cases?"

"You're right to suggest it might not be entirely selfless. I think I just might learn how to live again, learn what humanity is if I'm surrounded by any kind of vibrant life. Not only when I go into the streets, but here, and elsewhere, once I must leave this city. I've forgotten what it's like to live with someone."

"Is that why you go to clubs and parties? To try to feel?"

"Yes, though it's difficult with some things." He stares at Léon, and then his attention drifts down, and Léon follows his gaze; he's peering at the crucifix.

"But you always stand back. You don't partake. You never once even tasted the food."

He still can't believe that this man wants him, and how it awakens a fire in him. Léon isn't meant to be the main character; he's the disposable one. The erotic accent in an interesting person's life.

Matthias leans close. "And what if I wanted a taste?"

Shit.

This can't be happening. I don't, I don't...

"You've talked long enough," Léon mutters heatedly. "It gets dull after a—"

Matthias clutches Léon's shirt and yanks his forward until their lips and noses touch, and a dam breaks in Léon, and he closes the distance between them, heat exploding inside of him as he claws at Matthias' shoulders, but he can't kiss the other man deeply enough, even as their teeth clash and pain whitens his vision when Matthias' canines scrape open his bottom lip, and the hot copper-salt of tang of blood pours into his mouth.

Fuck his shame, his reservations.

Matthias releases a low moan, and then, too soon, the other man jerks away and leaves Léon open-mouthed and staring, as wetness trickles down his chin, and his chest burns—his hand shoots to his crucifix, and for some reason, it's hot, and Léon reflexively lets it go as he sees a whisper of smoke rising from a burn in Matthias' tunic.

And—

Léon steps back, staring at Matthias' mouth.

Mouth.

Eyeteeth.

Fangs.

"Dear God." His voice is a phantom of itself. "What's wrong with your teeth?"

"Wrong," Matthias echoes, his pupils dilated, his own lips brightened by Léon's blood. "Is that how you see it? See me?"

Matthias' eyes glow red.

Léon's stomach drops.

The dream with the red eyes.

That's not all.

Alongside his eyes and teeth, for the first time ever, his hair is tousled, and for the first time, Léon sees how his ears poke up, with an inhuman, elfin shape.

"Dear God, what are you?"

Matthias raises both hands, going forward. "Léon, I can explain—

Stumbling back, Léon bends and darts a hand down to his boot, at the sheath poking out. Claire's sweet voice, light as the wind, enters his mind.

Don't forget to take this, beloved.

She's always been more prepared than him for any setbacks.

When Matthias comes to close the distance between them, whether to kiss or kill him, Léon unleashes the knife and, with all his strength, shoves Matthias against the wine rack, pressing the blade to his throat.

Chapter 11

Léon

When Léon takes all his effort, even if it makes his spine pop, to shove Matthias against the wines, the bottles jostle but don't fall and shatter to the ground. He holds the knife to Matthias' throat, a pale column that he realizes has no flutter of pulse.

Infuriatingly, even threatened, Matthias gives a close-mouthed smirk and looks down. All that said, he's glad that this man of stone is now getting into the spirit. "This brings back memories. Did you know that the male lover I had was sent to kill me? Ah, my pretty little assassin."

Léon isn't sure if the dead lover is the pretty little assassin, or him. "Medium-sized, at least." He stares at those fangs, and he knows that it's a pipe dream—even if he's feeling faint and perspiring from not using his pipe tonight in an attempt to be normal—to think he could overpower Matthias. He's being humored, as if they're playing.

And Léon can't help but think that perhaps he did hit the pipe, and that he's lost his mind. He'll blink and realize he's delirious, and yet, Matthias isn't yelling, *Let me go! You've lost your mind!* In fact, it's as if they're both more awake than they've been in a long while.

Lightly, Matthias explains, "Your knife won't do anything to me. This doesn't need to be violent."

"You've *bitten* me."

"It was an accident. Let me go, and I'll explain."

"I don't believe you. Let me guess, you have no reason to kill me."

"Correct."

"What if I gave you a reason?"

A sigh. "Are we going to keep chasing our tails, but you're going to have a knife against my neck? I feel like this will get old."

It's then that Matthias' pupils change, rippling, but Léon can't say how or why, except that he feels sick.

Léon scrambles back. "God. What are you?"

Matthias strides forward and straightens his ruffled clothes. "Guess. You mentioned reading gothic novels. I'm not a ghost or a lycanthrope. There aren't many other options, my dear."

Léon's heart lurches.

A vampire.

He clutches his crucifix.

Léon tries to keep his voice from trembling, but he still sounds meek. "Is this a product of the lead you've tried to transfigure, my good alchemist? Has it driven you mad?"

"Use your eyes, Léon. You are rather close to me." His eyes fall distastefully to Léon's chest, at the silver crucifix dangling there.

Warily, Léon asks, "Can you not touch someone with something like this on?"

"I could touch you, but it'd hurt rather obscenely. I could—"

"Kill me? Yes, your seduction continues to work wonders *oh so* very well, darling. I'm positively vibrating." Léon cannot stop his voice from souring. "What happens if I take it off? What will you do?"

Matthias slips his hands into his pockets. "I don't have to do anything. As I said, I have no intention to hurt you, but you don't believe me. Given what I do know about what you've been through, I can't blame you, but it doesn't negate that I haven't lied to you. Only obfuscated a few details."

"I've lost the plot, and I think you have, too, if you ever had it."

All the evidence is before him. Matthias' unnatural poise and strange eyes. His pointed ears. The burned part of his tunic where the crucifix touched, seemingly reacting to when their skin touched. His baffling cravat he wore last night and at the burlesque club. Because for all the stylish opera cloaks in fiction, if anyone has an excuse to not understand fashion, it's someone born centuries ago.

Centuries. Matthias hasn't said as much, as much as he's said that he grieved for so long and was in a war that Léon doesn't know. "When were you born?"

"1497."

"Ah. Were cravats in fashion in Vienna?"

"No." Matthias tugs at his collar. "I like them."

"Oh, fine." Léon's blood roils under his skin. He should be terrified; he could die right now. But he's excited. Who wouldn't be, meeting someone who must know hundreds of years of art, poetry, science, and history? And to think, they already have such an interesting rapport. "If you are a vampire, prove it. Bite me. Again."

"What," Matthias replies flatly.

Léon surges forward, staring up at the other man. "You heard me. Drink from me."

"Please, I won't indulge your self-destructive habits."

Lowly, Léon replies, "Haven't you already?"

Matthias slips a handkerchief out of his pants pocket and hands it to Léon. It's a mere unadorned white cloth, and when Léon wipes at his mouth and chin, he rubs off flakes from the dark brown crust of blood.

Léon stares down at the handkerchief, taking a deep breath. This cloth in one hand, his knife in another, the sheath lying by the rack. "Believe it or not, I don't make a habit of asking strangers to bite me. Out of the many things I've done, I've never been interested in biting."

"Like you've never been interested in men," Matthias replies dryly. The utter audacity.

Léon folds up the handkerchief and hands it back. "Oh, hush."

He isn't afraid of Matthias. The statements of "I would've killed you if I wanted to" are about as reassuring as a coiled venomous snake in a lingerie drawer, but against all odds, Léon believes him.

"Do you want to taste my blood?" asks Léon.

"I already have."

"Do you want more?"

"I don't need it."

"That's not what I asked. Now, who's skirting the question?"

"I'm not sure if I want more of yours, specifically. Your blood tastes like everyone else's. There is no distinct flavor from one person to another."

"A chef can make the same meal a thousand times, and the customers will come for more of the same."

"I don't see you as food."

"But I can provide you with what you need."

"Anyone can."

"Can they? Is it the same drinking from me as it'd be with a stranger you bump into in the Parisian night? If it is, why not leave already?"

"This is my home."

"But you're thirsty, aren't you? Or hungry, however it works. Sorry, am I talking too much?" Léon sways his hips as he comes flush against Matthias' chest. "I don't have anything to stop me."

"Would you make me like you? Have you ever done that to anyone else?"

"I haven't."

"But you know how?"

"Yes. It was done to me."

"By whom? Was it the assassin?" When Matthias is quiet, Léon pushes, "Really? He tried to kill you *and* he turned you? How very dramatic."

"It was all rather complicated."

"Where is he now?" asks Léon, thinking that he might like to meet this man who's influenced Matthias' life this much.

Distantly, Matthias tells him, "My sire lost himself."

"I'm not certain what that means. How does a vampire lose himself?"

Matthias' gray eyes narrow. "Do you *ever* stop talking?"

Léon flutters his lashes. "I think I've been rather reserved, considering all that I've learned as of late. Will the, hm, feeding burn because of the crucifix?"

"Yes, for me, but don't mind that. After hundreds of years, I can handle a singed tunic." With that, Matthias' gaze flickers to the knife. "Are you going to let that go?"

"Probably not."

Matthias cups his jaw, thumb tracing a soft arc into Léon's cheek. "And yet, you'll let me bite you."

"You have your teeth, and I have mine. Of course, it'd be easier if Claire were here, since two sets of teeth nipping at someone's heels are better than—"

Matthias covers his mouth with his own, and this time, Léon darts his tongue against the man's lips, which have begun to swell, and he delights when he feels a prick of pain and tastes the mingling of smoke and blood. It's not so bad to be devoured.

And then, when Matthias pulls away, a string of blood and saliva breaking between them, his palms, thrumming—*were they always doing that? he always looks so frozen in time*—slide down to Léon's shoulder as he lowers his mouth and burrows it into the side of Léon's tender neck.

Chapter 12

Léon

With the first sting of teeth in his flesh, all of Léon's nerves sing. Not sure what to anticipate and how to act, he thrashes, and Matthias jerks his head back.

Annoyed, Léon says, "Go on. If I tell you to stop, keep going."

His mouth already stained red in a way that makes Léon go completely flush, Matthias replies in a raspy husk, "You must know I can't agree to that."

Léon scoffs as his entire body buzzes. He feels the cool cellar air on the heat of his open wound. "Oh, perfect, I've found the vampire with *morals*. Then, go, and I'll tell you if it becomes too much. Just don't scar my neck. It's one of my favorite features, besides my hair, face, and body."

Matthias doesn't need much prompting to continue, as he leans in, and as gently as someone can bite and suck, does so.

Léon moans and feels his groin stiffening and straining. A sensation flowers in him, from his throat to his chest to his limbs, a warm and throbbing and all-consuming flood, like that crest before sexual climax, but held like a tenuous bow on a taut cello string. He imagines his blood on Matthias' lips, making him fuller.

Their hearts are one; their souls are one, writhing and fluttering together at the pace of their united pulses.

He doesn't realize the exact moment when he's dropped the knife as he wraps an arm around to press Matthias even closer, but the weapon is gone. And what they're doing feels more obscene yet reverent than the most indulgent sex. Though pain radiates from where Matthias feeds, Léon feels complete having been able to give himself to someone in this way, this sticky mess between them.

He might be able to get used to it, but there's something missing. This night isn't enough.

He craves more.

Léon sleeps like the dreamless dead.

He doesn't remember the moment he goes to sleep. What he does remember is feeling faint and Matthias helping him sit against one of the casks.

"I'm fine," he had murmured, and it was true. Though his head was giddy, he knew it'd pass. Then, he shut his eyes for a small nap in what was certainly not the most uncomfortable position he's been in.

So when he wakes up, he doesn't know where he is, only notices as sunlight streams through a tall, narrow window with latticed iron and sullen vermillion curtains billowing to the red carpet. Léon groggily looks to his right, where the mantel burns low.

He blinks groggily and tries to orient his limbs. Yes, they're still attached, but they're lost in a velvety sea that is far too comfortable to swiftly exit from.

When he feels something stiff on the left side of his neck, he scrunches up his shoulders as a dull pain beats there, and he rises against the mountain of pillows behind him and lightly touches what's on his skin: a bandage.

He blinks again and takes stock of himself before he looks too deeply at his surroundings. He feels fine, though a little drained. He wonders if this is what a flower relieved of some of its nectar feels like.

When he gains the energy to sit up, he looks at his watch on his right wrist, and when he does, his heart leaps in shock.

Around 2:05...in the afternoon, by the looks of it.

It's not the first time either he or Claire has gone off, but usually they know when the other might be absent for the night and especially the next morning.

As he lifts off the covers, the sinfully soft sheets that almost frighten him when he thinks, *I could stay here forever.*

A plate of food rests on the nightstand, which is as dark as the rest of the furniture in the room. On the surface is a sliced pear and a chunk of brie, and beside that a mug of black coffee that, when he tastes it, is strong but cold. When he bites the cheese, it melts on his fingers and tongue, creamy and buttery.

I could get used to being served in bed.

Flipping back the tendrils of tousled hair in his face with his clean hand, Léon tries to recall how he got here, but as he does, his attention drifts past the dark mahogany floorboard with a rosy design to peer upon the framed painting.

The painting's a portrait of a man that ends just above his knees. He wears a white ruff and a black and gold surcoat with a sheathed curved sword—a saber?—at his hip, where he sets one hand. On his left breast is the silver design of a swirling dragon, its maw snapping open. Feathers of auburn hair fall on his shoulders, a more prominent mustache above his set lips.

And of course, those unmistakable gray eyes.

Did you carry me? Hold me? His chest suddenly feels strained.

When he does get up, unceremoniously licking savory flavor off his fingers, he can't find a mirror in the bedroom, but he finds one in the washroom. There are spots of blood on his collar, but he supposes it'd be a touch too far for Matthias to dress him and cocoon him in one of those stylish robes Léon covets. When he rolls the collar into the inside of his shirt, it doesn't look so bad.

He drifts through the rooms and finds an out of tune piano he idly plays. There's also a cello and even a harp. He also finds easels and blank canvases that Claire would love, since they have no room in their apartment for her to paint, but most of the other rooms are barren of even wallpaper.

To his disappointment, he can't find Matthias. Not even in the main hall, and when he looks

Wait, can vampires walk in the sun?

Maybe it's for the best. How foolish he might look if he shows gratitude.

I should make my leave and let Claire know I'm all right.

With little else to do, he leaves the estate and tries to find a taxi.

Once Léon realizes the rest of the world still exists, that's when life starts to sour.

He returns to find Claire being accosted on their apartment complex steps by a lumpy bratwurst of a man. His hair is brown, and he wears a sleeveless white shirt that reveals the bulk of his arms.

"I always wondered where you went, whore," the man snarls, gripping her arm.

"I'm sorry," Claire replies, schooling her expression and avoiding the towering man's gaze. "I don't know you."

Léon picks up his pace.

"The hell you don't. Who did you hire to do that to him, bitch?"

"I'm sorry, sir, I don't know what you're talking about. I don't know you."

"I'll have you gutted, whore. I promise to God I will—I'll have my men—"

Léon storms up to the man. "Friend, threaten her again and I swear—"

The man peers down at him with beady, watery blue eyes. "What will a little cocksucker like you do?"

With no other recourse, Léon throws a blow he knows will land badly, and it does, hitting a slab of chest; he'd be more successful trying to crack a brick with his bare knuckles.

In retaliation, as Claire claws at the man's arm, he slings it back and slams it into Léon's jaw; expectedly, Léon collapses on the steps.

"Hey!" a voice shouts. It's the taxi driver, an older man who's stopped and taken off his black cap. "What's happening here?"

The brute scowls, as more people stop to observe, and he lets Claire go. She flies down to where Léon is sprawled on the concrete. She reaches to help him into a sitting position against the banister.

The man points at Claire and growls, "I'll be back for you, and I won't be alone."

After, they sit on their ugly, old blue sofa, as Claire presses a cold washcloth to his aching jaw. He's insisted on checking the bruises on her arm, but she's brushed his hand away.

Léon jokes, "You know, maybe this time I'll look more like a hero and less like a mottled peach. Who was it, exactly, that I punched?"

Claire's mouth forms a hard line. "He was the brother of my old partner. You know, the one I stabbed fifty-seven times."

"Oh, silly, me, I thought it was fifty-eight." He hopes the dark joke will make her smile, but he sees her sinking deeper into herself, crossing her arms over her chest. "Did this brother, did he..."

"Do you think that my 'companion'"—her pimp—"kept me safe from his own brother?"

Léon's face twists in sadness. "Claire, I'm so sorry."

She gives a joyless smile and pats his hand. "Yes. Me, too." Her face floods with regret as she looks at his jaw, and her voice cracks. "God, I didn't mean for this to happen."

"Stop, I would face a thousand brutes like him for you. Even if it means I'd get my ass kicked a thousand and one times."

Claire stands and starts to pace.

With the draping fabric of her long, seashell-pink dress and a spiderwebbed lace collar with a pearl at the hollow of her throat, Claire looks like Salome long after her dance, when, hair tousled, she holds the saint's severed head aloft and kisses those dead, martyred lips.

She truly is the most beautiful woman he's ever seen.

Her face a map of dark worried lines, she presses her knuckles to her lips. She approaches the window to the right of the room, pensively looking out. "How was your night?"

"To tell you the truth, I slept through most of it."

Claire teases, looking over her shoulder with shimmering green eyes, "Was your experience that taxing?"

"Believe it or not, we didn't sleep together."

"Ah. Yet."

"Yet," Léon admits. "If that brute wants to cause trouble, Matthias might be able to shelter us from any danger."

Claire faces him with a hand on her hip, and Léon thinks of the painting in the bedroom. "What makes you think he would?"

We kissed, and then he drank my blood. We have history now.

"I think he likes us," Léon replies.

"And what would we tell him?"

"I told him what we both did."

A pregnant pause.

God, he's a fool.

"How much?" asks Claire.

"Everything."

Claire stares in disbelief before shaking her head. "Oh, God. *Léon.*"

Léon waits as Claire lowers her chin, her gaze half-lidded but crinkled around the edges.

"Dear God, dear God, dear God," she mutters.

Continuing to sit on the sofa, he says nothing because he can't exonerate himself, and he doesn't want to try.

Irritation flickers across her features, not that he blames her. "What gave you the right to tell him *both* of our secrets?"

Léon raises his hand. "Nothing. I'm sorry. It was wrong of me, and I wasn't thinking."

Her gaze pierces his. "He knows we killed the people who hurt us?"

"Yes."

She sucks in a deep breath.

"But he wasn't judgmental," Léon points out.

"Oh, good," Claire replies sharply. "At least there's that."

"There's more."

The space between her brows pinches, but her voice is weary. "What more could there possibly be?"

"I don't think Count Matthias is entirely human."

Another pause.

"Count? Not entirely human? Dear God, you can't stop there. Léon, what are you saying?"

Léon rubs his sore face. "Claire, my dear, you don't think I'm mad, so you?"

"I think everyone is a little mad. But generally, no. Just tell me."

So, Léon does.

"He's a vampire."

She stares.

"Do you mean he enjoys pretending to be one, or..."

"He drank my blood."

"That's a fetish I've never tried. Is that why you have that bandage on your neck?"

He gestures to his covered injury. "Yes. I felt, I felt—it wasn't normal. It wasn't a mere play for him. I wasn't just his plaything in that moment. Our hearts danced together. I don't know how to explain it."

She murmurs, "I'd say that speaks volumes."

"Here, look." With a discomfited grunt, he tears off the bandage and shows her his throat.

Claire's eyes widen. "God. Oh, Léon. Is there anything I can do?"

"It'll heal." A pause. "I think."

"Let's hope so! Are you sure it doesn't need to be cleaned?"

Léon offers a reassuring smile that doesn't seem to reassure her. "It'll be all right, but..."

"What is it?"

"Matthias says he wants to embrace me and make me like him."

"Like him. Are we talking about lurking in a castle and turning into a bat? Being one with wolves? I might like to have a wolf pack. But..." Claire doesn't speak for a long time. When she does, as he waits, she holds up a hand. "I'm not sure I can believe this."

He stands, and she sweeps to him. "Beloved, I'm telling the truth."

Heatedly, Claire replies, cupping the unhurt side of his jaw. "I know you are. I know you're not lying to me, but this is quite a lot to accept. A vampire? Like from those Victorian pulp novels? Those undead creatures with the bats and the capes?"

"Yes, more or less, though I haven't seen him in an opera cloak yet, but when he bit me, it was more than simple pain or pleasure. I saw, I felt a change. My crucifix, it burned him."

"I suppose if God exists, so, too, do damned creatures. Damned, undamned. Think about what we could do if Matthias is telling the truth."

"You're entertaining it?"

"Aren't you? I don't know, truly. I have to...I, I think I'd need to see for myself, but then again, I'm not sure I want to be around someone who drinks blood, who drank yours, even if you consented. But if he could change everything..."

"But you'd truly consider joining him?" Léon asks, truly curious and compelled to hear her reasoning. Because if she wants it, then surely, he isn't deluded.

"By God, yes, if what he's saying is true, you have a chance to escape the doldrums of life, this facade, you should do it. If I were you, even if I consulted you, in my heart, I would've already made my choice."

"Then, you can go to him. Maybe with me."

"Perhaps I will. Either way, I know we aren't safe here if we're going to start being watched and followed. We might as well have a patron."

"I know I'm not—"

Holding both her hands up, Claire snaps, "Stop. Don't start with the self-deprecation. I can't take it. I know you must've had your reasons for revealing everything to him in the moment. I know. Now, we must decide what to do next, and if he'll help us, I say we accept his terms. Far be it for me to deny the help of an attractive man with luscious hair."

Léon says passionately, "I want to be a good husband to you. I want us to have a good home and a family. I know I'm not able to do that now. That's not self-effacing. It's a mere fact. If the Count's offer were to change all that, I'd want to give you everything you deserve."

She purses her lips, eyes shining with unshed tears. "Oh, Léon. I do want a family. And a good home where we can sleep without worry."

"I regret that I haven't been able to give us those things. That I can't keep a job." And it's his fault. As much as Léon can joke about how most bosses are damned fuddy-duddies and just don't understand that he works best if he's a *little* drunk, even if he spills drinks every now and again, well, he's failed. In truth, he'd only gotten in one fight at a bar and broke one man's nose, and that was his sole trip to the big house.

"Listen to me," Claire whispers to him. "I love you as you are."

"And I love you as you are, too, but the last thing I want for you is to temper your ambitions." It's Claire's fire that stokes his own.

"Do you want the embrace, too?" she asks him.

"I...I think about it, but I'm not entirely sure how we'd be different."

"If we were more powerful, if we had a man like Matthias at our side, we'd be unstoppable. We'd never live in fear again. I would trade anything I had for that. To...to be more."

"Even your soul?" inquires Léon softly.

She doesn't miss a beat. "Of course. What else is it doing now but languishing? I can drink, eat, and fuck across the world without a soul."

"Hm, indeed. That's fair. I don't know if he'll accept both of us. I don't want you to be in danger. I'd never forgive myself."

Her lips crease in a sad smile. "My love, I'm in peril now. I've killed. I'm already damned, but I sure as hell won't make it easy for God or the Devil to catch me."

"What is it you said to me once—'two lonely souls burn brighter together'? What about three?"

Claire sweeps toward him and pulls him into a tight hug, her heart frantically thundering in pace with his own.

With her by his side, Léon knows his choice, and he feels content with it.

Chapter 13

Léon

After they take a taxi to the mansion in the late evening, as the sky glows blue-purple with a rosy-pink horizon, Matthias ushers them inside without even a pause to ask why they've come.

As he guides them to one of the rooms on the ground floor, Claire looks around, admiring the oil paintings of nymphs, goddesses, and golden-haired, pretty gods like Adonis, whose bright scarlet blood swirls into an ocean of roses and anemones. Léon drinks in her appreciation and wonder, assured that they're making a good decision, that this is the beginning of a grand new life.

When Matthias opens one door and they go through, Léon expects a row of coffins or a bat cave. Instead, the room, unlike the others, is brightly painted white, with rows of tables with a variety of papers, books, and rows of vials. There's even, near the windows, a metal surgery table that glints as the electricity sputters on. The entire front side of the room is lined from the ceiling to the floor with black latticed windows. The floor is tile, checkered black and white.

This must be his science room, as if Léon knows the first thing about science, as he inspects a test tube with an indiscernible clear liquid.

And, of course, like many of the rooms, as if they're in an old castle, there's a hearth with plush red sitting chairs to the far left of the room. What's different, it seems, is a stray scalpel lying on the glass coffee table in front of the fireplace. Both Claire and Léon sit in two adjacent, cushioned chairs, while Matthias' eyes rake from the circular bruises on Claire's arm to the blooming one on Léon's jaw. His face, like always, is stone, but his eyes blaze more furiously than the stoked fire.

"May I have a cigarette, please?" Claire asks Matthias, swinging one leg elegantly over another as she drapes her arms over her lap.

"Of course, Madame." Matthias, dressed like he was before, but without a single wrinkle on his clothes, fishes out a pack from his pants.

Claire laughs like the chime of small bells and waves a hand. "Oh, please. You make me sound like a matron."

He gracefully hands her a cigarette, and when she presses it to her lips, he takes a metal lighter and produces a small flame to light the tip. "Is that not the customary address?"

She takes a deep inhale, and then smoke unfurls from her nose and mouth, the room plumed with the scent of tobacco. "It is, but it *still* makes me feel older than I am. Simply call me Claire, please."

With both hands on his knees, Léon asks, "You're always awake in the evening and night. Can you even go out during the day?"

Matthias faces him, his limbs strangely stiff. "Yes, it makes me extremely fatigued, but I can if I must. That said, I prefer not to when I can work at night without any impediments." He comes close and leans. His pale fingers hover over the ugly growing bruise on Léon's jaw. When he speaks, his voice is deathly low. "Who did this to you?"

His tone sends an exquisite dark chill down Léon's spine.

Léon realizes that here, he feels invincible. Like no one will harm them here. Like he can be free. He can tell jokes that fall flat and fumble, and he'll be okay. An unusual feeling.

"Oh, I'm just a very popular fellow. Sometimes it's a kiss; other times it's a punch."

Straightening, arm falling to his side, Matthias frowns. "Be serious."

Léon grins wickedly. "Always, my darling."

Always one to slash through the veneer, Claire asks, "Is it true that you're a vampire? Immortal?"

Matthias turns, his profile almost saint-like when framed by flames in the growing night outside. "Yes."

Claire hums, taking another drag of the burning cig. "Good."

Léon pipes up, "We were attacked by..." He takes a deep breath, inhaling wood smoke.

She finishes, "By the brother of my old pimp. I've been told you know all about that."

Matthias frowns. "He's the one who injured you both?"

"Yes," Claire murmurs, and her quiet is so pointed that Léon knows that she has a plan. "And when he comes for his revenge, I have no doubt he'll bring help, and it'll be long and slow." Whenever she has her mind on something, she narrows in on it with calm intensity.

Her posture was leaning against the chair arm, but she straightens, flicking the cigarette ash in a crystal tray. "Would you let a group of angry men carve us to pieces? They'd do even worse before we die."

Her words slice through the air like a cold knife. Matthias stands between them, his gray eyes soaking up all the light from the fire and the incoming moonlight.

"If you choose, you both are mine, and I am yours. I would never forsake you. To do so would be a mark of unforgivable dishonor."

The heated promise in his words frightens Léon, even as the tremble in him isn't entirely unpleasant. Good things don't last. And they're so close to having a home. One where they can sleep without fear.

Claire replies to that proclamation with startling clarity, crushing the cigarette in the ashtray. "I trust no one if they use only words. Prove it."

This has been her careful design, and Léon loves her for it. He can't pretend that they aren't both a little selfish. Never before have they been this close to safety and even power.

"My dear, you don't deserve to live in fear of vengeful men."

Gripping the armrests, Claire challenges, "How do you know what I deserve? I've barely spoken to you."

Matthias meets her gaze evenly, his eyes half-lidded, and yet he doesn't feel as guarded as he once did. "I can't say how I know, except when I look into your eyes. The dreams inhibited by life and mortality. The cunning. You deserve to be draped in a pearl necklace and furs."

Maybe I'd like to wear pearls and cravats and maybe even a fancy dress or two, something taffeta and damasque, because why not? I'm a man, but the way I can be a man is up to me.

Léon bursts into the conversation as he usually does: "Is she the only one who gets pearls and furs; I'd like a good necklace, especially if I can no longer wear my crucifix."

He palms his necklace. *God, You'll still love me, won't You? You won't forsake me if I'm different, will You?*

Matthias tells them both, setting a hand under his collar. "You can have whatever you want."

Standing, Claire glides toward Matthias, her draping pink dress shuddering as she moves. She meets his gaze, unabashed. "Talk is cheap, Count. Show me my pearls. Show me my final revenge."

Léon stands there, stunned, mesmerized by the deathly beauty of his wife. Already prepared for what might come next. He hopes he can be as brave as her.

Claire and Matthias are both swords, and Léon—he's not sure what he is. Lace and poppies. He just wants to lounge around and smoke and fuck and be fucked and make barbs. He's not sure he wants to kill. Even when he was at war, he was a terrible soldier, much better at holding a wine glass and a pipe and a conversation than a gun and bayonet.

That said, he can't help but think that if Claire would want to kill the remaining man, or men, who plague her, he'd happily be by her side.

Cruelty can be fun, after all. The rightly placed barb and such. You're not supposed to think so, but it's true. if it weren't, maliciousness wouldn't be so common. And, well, they're due some meat.

Léon palms the turquoise blanket on the arm of the chair, its color shockingly out of place amid the sea of reds, whites, and blacks.

Matthias cuts his attention from Claire, who blazes her intent into him. "I made that myself."

Léon halts and looks down at the blanket. "Pardon me, you *knit*?"

Matthias smoothly waves Léon off. "You don't need to sound so surprised. I'm a vampire, not a bore."

"Léon knits, too," Claire murmurs.

Matthias nods, taking the information in, but then he turns away from them both, once again soaking in the fire. "Tell me what you need to know."

Claire looks at Léon, who still sits. He sees the thoughts turning in her mind. So much, and yet, if they are so certain, there's not much to ask at all.

Léon pipes up. "What—will we be so different from how we are now? If vampirism is a kind of damnation."

"For the most part, no," Matthias replies, "but I have a monster in me."

"A dragon?" asks Léon. He remembers the sigils he's seen on the walls, the design on the oil portrait.

"Not quite. I can't explain it."

That's when Léon gets up and passes Claire to stand beside Matthias. And then Claire is on the other side of the Count as Léon reaches out and takes Matthias' steel grip into his own. "Try."

As Matthias stares into the fire, his chin low, Claire also eases her hand on Matthias', as his fingers hang by his sides.

"We creatures of the night have an insatiable need for blood, and we must restrain it while giving in enough to feed. When you *kill*, you begin to lose yourself, go feral. You become powerful, but you also become less human. If you ignore that darkening, that eclipse, and keep indulging in bloodlust without care for who you kill, it consumes you, and you change permanently into a monster. It's not only a moral change. It's physical. It's—even that is too shallow. Death devours your soul."

Léon's eyes flicker to one of Matthias' pointed ears: "Have you gone through that change, like your sire?"

Matthias' voice is a deep rumble in his chest. "I was terribly close, but I pulled back. If I did cross that threshold, you wouldn't be speaking to me because a vampire who loses themselves cannot change back at will; they're forever monstrous. I can, at will, I can shift, but if I were to lose control and take someone's life without bringing them back, I might lose myself for good. That is, until I'm put out of my misery."

Claire asks, "Who would be able to do that?"

Matthias is silent for a long time. Léon imagines he must've thought of a scenario a thousand times over the centuries where he tracked down his lover and ended him; but he didn't.

Once he speaks again, his whisper is barely audible over the pop and crackle of the flames in front of them. "It'd take quite a lot of strength to slay a gaunt, a feral vampire who's lost forever. I doubt a mere mortal could do it."

Léon insists, "How do you know it's forever? Is there no cure? Surely, that'd be preferable." It hurts his heart to think of Matthias needing to kill someone he loves, should the moment ever arise.

"I've never known anyone to come back from the brink once they've pushed past it. I know for me, I must always have restraint. His eyes fall on Léon. No matter who tries to push me."

Claire lowers her head in thought.

Léon holds up a hand with a sheepish grin. "I don't know what you're trying to imply. I can't recall anything I've done that'd make you even a little murderous." He gestures to the side of his face. "Is that why your ears are, you know?"

Matthias regards him dryly. "Yes, if you must know. It's also why my hair changed color. Or lost color, however you want to put it."

Claire asks, "Do you know how to kill a gaunt, besides it needing a lot of strength?"

"I'm not entirely sure. Much like a vampire, or really, a regular person, I imagine that you must stab through the heart.

However, with a gaunt, it's a difficult task, because of how agile and big they are."

Agile. Big. Léon likes those. The mass homicide might be a problem, though.

Claire shifts her head to look at them both through her long eyelashes. "Is it, is it such a terrible thing when you're on the verge, if you can shift?"

Matthias replies, "It has its uses. I don't get any door-to-door salesmen or zealots." Léon can't tell if he's serious. On one hand, it doesn't sound like Matthias would be reckless with revealing his most inhuman form; on the other, it's a hilarious image.

Claire bats her long, dark eyelashes. "May I see your more monstrous form? At least, what you're able to become."

Matthias' voice takes on a rough, uneven cadence. "I know if you saw that, you'd run."

"You know," Léon says, "I doubt that. I might soil myself as my hands fly to my face and I shout, 'Oh, dear me!' But it'd take a great deal to frighten me enough to make me run."

Claire's eyes are bright, perhaps with furious tears. "I've had to hold fingers and feet as a physician sawed through men to save them. Don't assume what I can handle."

Though Léon does his damnedest to cool his expression, he's in awe of her sheer gall. No envelope she'll leave unpushed.

Matthias insists, squeezing both of their hands tenderly. "This is more than mortality. Promise me you won't ask that of me again. If I give you respect, you must reciprocate it in kind."

Claire lowers her head and gazes into the fire. "You're right. My apologies."

Matthias shakes his head, his voice low. "No, no apologies."

Léon asks, leaning in and lacing his voice with insinuation. "What do you want instead?"

Matthias meets his eyes, and though he's taller than them both, their lips are close enough to almost kiss. "I wasn't under the impression that you both came here because you wanted to hear about what I want. In fact, I think that's already been a topic of conversation. On the contrary, I thought it was about what *you* two want."

Claire then turns and clutches the space above Matthias' elbow. Léon can feel the heat brimming between all of them. "You know what we want. So, why keep us waiting?"

Matthias pauses, and then straightens, as if drawing in a breath. "Come, let's sojourn in my bedroom."

Chapter 14

Léon

Matthias' bedroom is as contradictory as he is. It is grand but austere. The colors are dark, gray, black, and maroon, but it's bright with firelight, as if Matthias is accustomed to living in large castles and seeks to ward away mildew. And, well, castles are stone, and here, the walls are stone covered with red rose wallpaper. There are, of course, no mirrors among the dark furniture, including a giant wardrobe and a writing desk, though Léon thinks that it might be nice to have one, if he were to see himself taken by Matthias with only his own reflection in the glass.

Léon's not sure what's come over him, but he likes it. He likes how his neck wound still stings, a promise of more to come.

With Claire by his side, looking at a bookshelf of poetry, of the Romantics and Baudelaire, Léon gives a sweeping gesture to the hearth. Matthias stands by the end of his bed, which is terribly immense for one person, with plum-purple sheets and a matching canopy, the fabric appearing so soft that it puts the den of pleasure's beds to shame.

As he regards, Matthias Léon coyly circles a finger around one of his curls. "It must be a terrible pain in the ass to have to light all these fireplaces on your own."

"I know all about pains in the ass, and this one is a small price to keep a bed warm."

Léon brushes back some of his locks. "Ha! Oh, I know other ways to keep a bed warm. I thought you'd sleep in a coffin."

"Yes, I do," Matthias admits. "Most of the time."

"Where is it?" Claire asks, turning from the bookshelf by the fire.

"It's in a chamber below," Matthias replies, crossing his arms and staring into the flames by a lion-clawed velvet plush chair.

Léon asks, "Are there little statues of bats? Or real bats?" At the other man's severe look and Claire's small laugh, Léon pouts.

Matthias snaps his fingers and looks at Claire while he points to Léon. "Does this one ever stop with the barbs?"

Claire takes Léon's hand and presses a kiss to his cheek. Always his darling. "I'm afraid not." He can see Matthias taking them both in, and Léon imagines it must be strange to be the odd one out, the addition to an established relationship.

Léon teases Matthias, "You're just far too masculine to admit that you like it."

Matthias sniffs. "I'm not sure what you mean. You could've stood to have made up the bed before you left."

Léon balks. "The guest, expected to clean up after themselves? What has the world come to? Anyhow, on to the more important questions: Can you turn into a bat?"

"Why do you ask? Of course I can."

"That might be useful, but I really feel as if I'd look better as a nightingale, with my lyrical voice. Or a sparrow."

Matthias replies flatly, "That's what you're concerned about."

He squeezes Claire's hand. "Why *wouldn't* I be concerned about shapeshifting? That seems like something pivotal to think about. Being able to change into something is a powerful motivator, but if the only thing I could turn into is a blowfish, I'd be disinclined to accept."

"I doubt whatever forces decide what you'll turn into would have you blow off even more air than you already do."

Whatever forces. Léon doesn't know. If Matthias doesn't know what supernatural forces altered him, how can they learn?

Satan, perhaps, but even the devils are instruments of God. They wield misery to lead mortals to righteousness. Job only loved God the most when his children, home, and health were taken from him.

Is that what we'll do, bring more misery and damnation into the world? And for what?

Part of him thinks that, well, he doesn't want to, but perhaps this is the price of safety for himself and the one he loves. The world would have them die and no longer inconvenience it. Fuck that, and fuck the world. Immortality is proof they survived despite being told that they shouldn't because they aren't untraumatized or sweet or pure enough.

But he hopes that should they change they aren't truly damned. God works in mysterious ways, and surely he wouldn't let his followers defy death if there weren't a reason, good or ill.

Matthias doesn't seem to be like that—an unholy creature. Léon doesn't feel sad or afraid around him, except when he feels this near-tangible longing of a man displaced from a home that no longer exists. Budapest and all of Hungary, no matter the shifting country lines, still exist, but it can never be as it was in the fog of childhood. Léon still remembers plum-pleasant memories of home because his life became grief and being pleasing to others and terror. Being smaller and smaller, a shrinking glass bottle of swelling water.

Claire then interrupts them, her voice carrying a somber husk. "Can vampires conceive?"

"It's incredibly rare. I've never known anyone who has given birth after death. The...the process works, but there's not much to lead to fertility. It's almost like menopause, and the semen, well." Matthias makes a loose gesture with his hand.

"It's like shooting blanks?" Léon suggests.

Matthias sits at the edge of his bed, while they remain standing between the door and the fireplace, and Léon wants nothing more to be there with him. "Yes. Most of the time. At least, much more than—or less than, depending on your perspective—than mortals."

"Why is that?" Claire asks.

"I don't know. The sources I've read have given it a one in a million chance, but that's all."

Claire raises a brow. "The vampire encyclopedias?"

"There's an occult school called Scholomance in the Southern Carpathians of Transylvania, where there are many esoteric texts barred from most of the world. That was how I learned more about my condition. But, as you might expect, there aren't extensive scientific studies done on vampire pregnancies."

Claire shares a pensive look with Léon. "One in a million. I see."

It's a conundrum. Léon always imagined having a family, but then he thinks, well, who'd want someone like him as a father? Aren't fathers meant to be burly and emotionally detached? That's how his papa was. Léon's dramatic; he's an addict; he loves too much in a way that makes his head dizzily giddy.

And if they were to join Matthias, part of him thinks that they might be able to do that without the immortal kiss. So they could have him *and* the chance of a family.

But then he thinks of the ability to live forever and experience so much. To transcend. To have that power to fight back and protect those he loves.

Matthias looks between the both of them. "If that's a concern, I understand. I would never want to get in the way of your ability to have a family. I know that when I was mortal, I was always at war, always planning and absconding rest, that I neglected that part of my life."

Claire nods, clasping her hands before herself before giving a little hum. "If I want to make my own legacy, there are other ways to do it. There are other ways to have a family."

Other ways. She's right. One need not have blood relations to have a family. After all, she's his closest family yet.

Matthias inquires with utmost seriousness, "Do either of you have any family left?"

"No," Claire says quietly, nestling her hand to her collarbone.

"I was the fourth of six sons," Léon says. And the prettiest, hence why his endearing Maman and Papa sold him to a brothel when he was sixteen. He had none of the shine of his little brothers and none of the true right to exist like his three eldest brothers. "But I left my old life a long time ago. We weren't close, and I wouldn't know how to find them as I tried.

"What were your brothers' names?"

Jules, Louis, Nicolas, Marc, Paul.

Léon looks away from both of them, unblinking. "I can't say I remember. My parents made unremarkable children, except for me, as we know. And then, when my parents died, we scattered. My older brothers tried to keep us together, but I ran away."

In truth, Léon couldn't stand to be even close to the room where his mother wheezed and choked on her own blood, where he cleaned up her spittle and piss and tears. He couldn't help but feel as if he were haunted in a way that his crucifix couldn't protect.

Besides, he was a menace to his eldest brothers, always sulking and scowling and throwing fits and running off. They must've breathed a sigh of relief when he disappeared one night and never returned.

Claire crosses her arms over herself. "I never had any siblings. I think I might've liked to have at least one, so I could've had someone to relate to. But I've found there are ways to connect to others more than you've ever felt for someone you share blood with." She never spoke much about her childhood or home life, and Léon never pressed. He imagined if it was that terrible that dredging it up would only hurt her more.

Claire holds Matthias' gaze, and Léon watches as the moonlit air simmers between them. What he'd give to read their thoughts. Léon isn't even sure if Matthias likes women, though he remembers at least one of the looks Claire and Matthias shared when they had their night of indulgence.

Léon has been concerned that Matthias and Claire might not get along; at least, maybe not as well as he and Matthias have, but then again, they haven't known the vampire for long, and he's still reeling from how much sense it *does* make to think, *My companion, the vampire.* Vampires, which exist, and it's fine, really, because being Matthias' bloodslut once was actually rather nice that one time.

Nevertheless, the last thing he wants is to drag Claire into an arrangement she doesn't want, but as Claire toes off her pumps and crosses the distance between her and Matthias and straddles his lap, Léon realizes that it'd be difficult for him to make Claire do anything. It's not in him to inhibit her. And the last man who tried before his idiot brother learned the price from his heart herself.

Gripping Matthias' shoulders, as those steely eyes drink her in, Claire cranes her head back to look at Léon out of the corner of her eye, her voice a lowered husk rasping alongside the fire. "Have you two kissed?"

"Yes," Léon answers.

She then looks at Matthias again, and Léon wishes he could discern her look, but he can only see the crown of her head. "I think it's a shame. Léon and I have been together, you two have had your time, but both of us haven't had any fun. And you were so patient when we were with Henri."

With that, she rises to claim Matthias' mouth and a kiss, making a small noise as his arms snake around her waist and clasp her close. She shudders in his grasp, and Léon can't help the burgeoning prick of arousal, content in the sight. The idea of sharing one man. And the thought that Claire will experience what he has—the thrill of being bitten and losing herself in orgasmic delirium.

It feels right, the three of them, as if they're fated.

When Claire deepens the kiss, her shoulders noticeably taut as Matthias' fingers dig into the fragile fabric of her dress, she shivers again and moves her head and throat back, as if preening to show Matthias her exposed pulse. "Mm. You taste like cinnamon and metal."

"Thank you," Matthias replies. "I try."

Claire laughs, and then, running her hands through her short hair, she orders, "Lie down." She tugs down her lace collar.

To Léon's delight, Matthias complies, his hands gliding over Claire's hips as he gets on his back, legs hanging off the side of the bed. It's interesting, even as Léon stands by the fireplace, now in the position of the observer, watching Matthias take this position. No longer is he at a distance, and the wound on the left side of his neck throbs, as if it too seeks release.

She gets off him and sits beside where he rests prone. As she leans over with a sly smirk, Léon admires her, that smile that was once so faded, those curves that were once narrowed, her hips having jutted painfully out.

In the hot glow of the flames and moonlight, Claire runs her finger from the hollow of his throat to his chest to his navel. As Matthias is remarkably still, death-like, she makes quick work of unclasping his belt and unbuttoning his trousers. Léon considers that this man must be at least part-dead to not already be noticeably stiff. He wonders if the man, deep down, is a little shy.

Léon cannot help but step forward, transfixed. He might be mad, but though Matthias isn't looking at him, he can feel the man's burning thoughts on him, and he feels the weight of centuries of eschewing intimate engagements. He's letting himself go and relinquishing control. If Matthias weren't undead—if Léon hadn't felt the weight of hundreds of years in his heartbeat—his own heart might be loud enough for Léon to hear.

When Claire frees Matthias' cock, it's indeed partially erect as Claire gently uses her fingers to raise the tip close to her lips. Gripping the base of him and tenderly unsheathing his foreskin, Claire rolls her tongue over the top of him. She then darts out her tongue to dance circles around him before taking more of him into her mouth.

As her head motions up and down, her hair partially falls in her face until Matthias raises himself on his elbows and reaches to push it away from her eyes. His expression is inscrutable, all except for the scorching intensity in his eyes. It certainly makes sense that, between the two of them, Claire was the first to brazenly go this far with Matthias.

Léon goes to join them—

But first, after removing his jacket and placing it on a gilded chair, he reaches behind his neck, under his curtain of golden curls, and searches for the clasp of his necklace. It's been a long while since he's taken it off, no matter what extravagance he's engaged in.

He then removes his shoes and approaches the bed, sitting on the other side of Matthias. Though Claire keeps holding Matthias' length, she pauses her ministrations to look up at him through half-lidded eyes. In what might be considered an amusing gesture, Léon simply stares between Matthias and Claire, doing everything but scratching his head despite knowing how to suck cock, as a professional. Really, he's a connoisseur of fellatio.

Léon gives a closemouthed grin to his wife and his...companion. "Forgive me, my mind is parsing the difference between having sex near a man and having sex with a man. I'll be fine." It feels odd that he still hasn't fully embraced that perhaps his attraction to men wasn't a mere formality when he needed francs, but hopefully, he won't be mocked.

Raising a hand, Matthias tells him, "You don't need to do anything." Even being pleasured on his back, he maintains that air of composure.

Léon makes a show of straightening his shirt and flipping his hair behind his shoulders. "Well! Certainly, I'm not letting you two have all the fun. I might not be the jealous sort, but I do get a little jealous when others are having climaxes, and I'm not." He is, however, straining in his pants; not everyone can have Matthias' restraint.

So, with his usual drama, Léon rolls his shoulders and leans down, careful not to bash his head against his wife's, which would rather hurt.

And, setting a hand on the rumpled fabric of Matthias' trousers, Léon runs his tongue along the length, as Claire joins him and sucks on the tip. Léon takes in the faint, sharp salt of him, alongside the hint of smoke and brimstone in his nostrils.

Matthias' careful façade begins to unravel with the rasp of two tongues dancing on his sensitive skin. Léon's pulse is a frenzied bird fluttering in his throat.

Eventually, as they take turns laving Matthias' cock, the vampire gets into the sitting position and motions for them to stop. Overwhelmed when he looks into Claire's desire-brimmed green eyes, they shift closer to the pillows and rest on their sides to kiss, her hands threading through his hair as he opens his mouth to deepen their necking as he traces a thumb along her jaw.

As they kiss, tasting the salt of saliva and pre-come, Matthias bends between Claire's long legs, which are spread at an angle, her dress pooled around her navel, and dips his mouth to her. She gasps into Léon's mouth, her nails digging into his neck as her lips part in delight, her spicy floral perfume tickling his nose.

When they break the kiss, she calls to Matthias, "Please, please, get inside me."

He raises his head above her pubis and says with comic seriousness, "Aren't I already?"

Claire gives a little scoff as she sits up and begins to shove her arms into her dress to shrug it off. "You know what I mean." After Léon helps her pull her dress over her head, she crawls to Matthias and helps him tug off his pants, revealing well-muscled calves that Léon can't help but admire the shape of. In fact, when both of them are unclothed, he can't help but rise and watch them.

Matthias sits cross legged on the bed, facing the headboard as Claire positions herself in the same direction while she climbs atop him.

Léon joins them, sitting on his knees before Claire and wiping the hair from her face, damp with perspiration; as she peppers his mouth and chin with kisses, he reaches down and helps join them. Despite his lack of release, he takes immense joy in the united, single convulsion of his partners when he glances Matthias' tip over Claire's clit before sliding him in. When Matthias starts to move, despite the uncomfortable position, Léon raises himself as Claire clasps his jaw fervently. Matthias' fingers rove the column of Claire's throat, as blush spreads across her chest.

"Léon," she whispers, throaty but quiet as a hymn, as she swallows his lips with her own, and he steadies her as she rides Matthias at an increasing pace. The heat of her pressed against him nearly drives him into a frenzy, and he's all too aware of Matthias' disheveled presence, the tallest among them, as Claire breaks off this kiss of passion and teeth, and Léon glides his chin over her shoulder and captures Matthias in a thorny kiss.

However, despite the wild moment, Matthias seems to be restraining himself, keeping himself from biting Léon as he clumsily reaches up, brushing Claire's arm and caressing the side of Léon's face as he tries not to deepen the kiss.

But Léon is hungry, eager to taste his own blood, to be swallowed. Hell, if he sucked Matthias' part, it's only fair that a part of him is sucked, right?

Nevertheless, unsated, he pulls away, not wanting to force something Matthias isn't yet ready to give again. Instead, feeling cunning, he leans back and then lowers himself on all fours, stretching out on his side and leaning close to where Claire and Matthias are joined.

Opening his mouth, Léon offers a long, languorous lick over where they meet, tracing Claire's clit before teasing the outline of her damp core and gripping the base of Matthias, who tantalizingly stops as he glistens, and Léon tastes the commingling arousal dripping down his shaft. He feels Matthias tense, and—

When Claire shudders, her arousal and pearly come gushing down Matthias' cock and on to Léon's tongue, he laps it up before rising to catch her. She digs her teeth and chin into Léon's shoulders and her nails press into his back. She tenses against him until her grip loosens, her hands snaking to come between them, and as he gently wraps his fingers over hers, another hand—Matthias'—almost shyly grazes against the fabric of Léon's shirt, and he grasps the man, too, so both their hands are joined above his heart in this brief moment of quiet.

After their first round, Claire excuses herself to go to the bathroom, to care for herself to reduce the risk of a kidney infection, which could lead to death.

With her gone, Matthias and Léon sit in the center of the bed, Léon balancing himself on his legs, curled beneath him, and his palms. They share a long look as searing as the fire.

"Think you have more in you?" Léon asks wryly.

"Oh," Matthias says lightly, his eyes shrewd. "I could go all night."

"That's impressive. All right." Léon pulls his shirt over his head. "My turn."

Matthias rakes his eyes over Léon's bare chest, which is certainly not quite as broad as his. "What do you want me to do?"

"Enter me. Please. I trust you to make sure it doesn't hurt. At least, not the sex."

That's not all, obviously. He needs Matthias to make him his bloodslut again. This achingly close, his arousal starting to feel more like a sting, he can see how his companion's pupils have swelled, working to consume the gray.

"Well then, show me how you want it done." A more delicate fashioning of *Get into the position.*

So, like a flower, Léon wilts, lying on his back with his arms languidly outstretched. It's then that Claire returns, still nude, and she climbs into the bed to lounge on her elbow beside Léon, stroking his jaw and neck as Matthias retrieves a vial from the nightstand, and when he positions himself between Léon's spread legs, uncaps the vial, and douses his fingers with the rosy-smelling oil, he lowers his hand and presses one digit at the entrance of Léon's ass. Léon's breath hitches as Claire coaxes her hand on his chest, soothing him when Matthias inserts another finger inside him. Then, she sits up, her hand trailing lower, and lower.

Léon moans while Matthias' nimble fingers stretch him and Claire strokes his neglected, leaking cock, and it takes all his strength not to climax right then, especially when Matthias spreads his fingers. Léon's fists twist into the sheets, as Claire starts to bend, but Matthias raises his free hand.

"No, wait. I want his pleasure."

With a pleased smile, Claire accepts what Matthias says, releasing Léon, who's straining not to burst.

When he's ready, Matthias rises and settles over him, bracketing his arms around Léon, who's all but ready to scream for Matthias to enter him.

"It's okay, beloved," Claire soothes Léon, taking his hand. "Breathe."

And then, the first thrust, barely an inch in at first, and then another, deeper, and a sudden, near-violent surge of pleasure rushes over him while, in the light of the fire and moon, he watches Matthias face contort, his eyes grow soft as he looks down at one of his new lovers.

Léon grunts and murmurs, "Pull my hair. Go on. Do it now."

Matthias obeys, one hand forming a hard knot in the hair on the side of his head. He relishes the delicious tug on his scalp, the completeness of controlling and being controlled. Because even here below Matthias, Léon knows that the other man is letting a part of himself, frightened and locked away, go as they couple.

Nevertheless, Léon squirms, restless in his lack of climax.

The hand that isn't hard as iron in his hair cups his cheek, and Matthias chest ruts against his. "Good, you're doing very good now, Léon." The friction of Léon's erection against Matthias' warm, thrumming skin almost sends him over the edge, but he remembers what Matthias said: *I want his pleasure.*

Dear *God.*

Léon can't help the mess of syllables and un-dainty curses that spill from him. He's lost sight of Claire, but he swears she's running her hands through his hair, and it's only then, the awareness of her, that he gets the strength to form a few coherent words.

Léon murmurs to Matthias, rolling through another deep plunge into him, "Bite me." Matthias regards him through half-lidded eyes. "Do you want me to beg? Bite me, please. Bite me, now."

With a growl, Matthias buries his nose and mouth against Léon's neck and clamps down, hard. The broken skin stings, and Léon moans in twined agony and ecstasy as Matthias laps at the re-opened wound, as it floods into his ready mouth. As Léon feels his pulse in his head, and the trickle of blood leaving his flushed throat, he's too aware of the rampant cadence of Matthias' relentless pounding.

Before Matthias can fully move away, Léon shifts his chin and kisses him, his mouth flooding with the tang of his own blood. And then Claire leans over them, too, and she kisses Matthias, drinking him in.

When he's done feeding, Matthias rises, settling himself deeper into Léon as his rhythm quickens, and Léon's hardness is angry and red. He's caught between a feeling of unreality, giddily drunk off the feeding and the metallic taste of his own blood, and Matthias has never looked more bestial, his gray eyes glowing.

Léon is utterly lost in reverie, lost in companionship. How could he ever think he's alone again?

Dazed and in a mix of pleasure that eclipses his desire for someone to give him his own completion, he looks over to Claire beside him. A dribble of blood has fallen on the silken cream of her breasts that he has the urge to lick away. She kneels, her fingers working into her soaked pussy; he's desperate to taste her again, so he calls hoarsely, "Claire, come here, let me, let me..."

She comes to him, and at his lazy motion, she offers a wry smile and swings her legs over his face, lowering herself so he can lick and please her. When she arches her back, her pussy dips lower for him to taste, his tongue circling her swollen clit as he feels her on the verge of another crest of pleasure.

And then, he feels a dam give, and Matthias makes a sound between a growl and a gasp as he gives a deep thrust that's almost painful, and heat floods Léon, and he basks in his wife's pleasure when she cries out, and he helps her ride another tide of pleasure.

And then, when Claire gets off him, he feels Matthias leave him void of all but that damp heat, and blearily, trying to stave off exhaustion, Léon watches as the man bows down, and a spike of pleasure erupts when Matthias gingerly sinks his mouth around Léon's tip; the light graze of fangs sends a hard jolt of pleasure as Matthias takes him deeper into his mouth, leaving a wet trail when he moves back up. And it's only Claire holding one hand that keeps Léon from thrashing when he arches and comes in deep spurts into the hot cavern of Matthias' mouth. The man grips him and strokes out every last drop, effortlessly swallowing.

On his back, Léon whispers to Claire, "Mon coeur, are you spent yet?"

"No," she says lightly, coaxing her thumb on his temple. "I think I have at least one more in me."

Raising his head, Léon asks Matthias, "If you were inside her, do you think you could take me inside you?" His heart is in his throat at the idea. From the sheer decadence of it, from the vulnerability he's showing, divulging his fantasy.

Pushing his hair from his face, Matthias replies, "I'm not sure, but I'm willing to try."

Chapter 15

Léon

Both Claire and Matthias help Léon to his knees; though he's not as exhausted as he was the previous night and the previous feeding, despite exerting himself far more, the bite makes him feel a little wobbly.

"Are you sure you're able to do this?" Matthias asks, gingerly clasping both of his shoulders.

"Yes. I'm not sure how useful I'll be after this, but I can manage this much, at least. I've done plenty of more strenuous bed acrobatics in my lifetime." And those hadn't been anywhere as fun. It's nice, when he lazily falls into Matthias' arms for no other reason than because he can, and Claire wraps her arms around his back; Matthias tentatively embraces them both, and they stay like that for a few warm minutes, cradling one another in a mass of flowers, smoke, and blood.

Never alone again.

Léon turns to meet his wife's mouth in a slow, tantalizing kiss. He's reluctant to part from this trinity they have, but he can't resist being ensnared in Claire's arms when she pulls him down with her, his fingers feathering in the velvety corona of her hair. When he pulls away, he nuzzles his nose against hers, and she leans up to press kisses against his throat.

She laps at his achy neck wound, and he already feels himself growing hard with pleasure as stinging arousal needles from his injury to every nook of his body. All their mouths are sticky with his blood, and that only augments his joy, that idea of being inside the both of them, of being consumed.

The pressure she applies to him starts off gentle, but it's harder for her teeth to penetrate his skin. She spreads her legs under him, and he trails his arms down to brace himself on both hands above her, and he nudges himself inside her as she licks at him, sending twinges across his skin while he feels Matthias closing in behind him, behind the tangle of limbs.

As Claire's wet heat surrounds his length, his cock twitches when he feels Matthias just barely enter him. The sensation of being in Claire while having Matthias reach deep inside him, stroking one of the most intimate parts of himself, almost makes him collapse on top of his wife before they've gotten too far. He relishes the tickle of Matthias hair on his back and his shoulder as Claire's chest is flush against his, her mouth by Léon's ear. She leans her head back, then, exposing her neck, and understanding what she wants, squeezed between them, Léon does his best to move his shoulder out of the way when Matthias leans down, their closeness the most it's ever been, and bites Claire's neck.

Claire gives a gasp, her legs jumping up to cage Léon's hips, her nails delectably scrabbling his sides. The smell of her blood rises, and his mouth waters; never before has he cared about the taste or scent of anyone's blood; it just was. If anything, it only reminded him of war, mingling with gunsmoke, mustard gas, and rot. But now, he can feel Matthias' eternally hungry heart throbbing against his spine, and Claire's pulse like a hummingbird beating a tattoo in his ribs.

"More," she murmurs, and Léon doesn't know if she means the fucking or the biting. "More." Though his movement is inhibited, Léon obliges, driving himself to thrust quicker in the haze of autumnal fire and blood, as she clenches around him.

Claire

When the three of them collapse in a pool of sweat and come and blood, with Léon shifting beside her, and Matthias against his back, Claire seashell-curls into herself, spent, as a dull pain radiates from her throat. She almost dozes off, Léon's palm pillowing her cheek. She drinks in his blue eyes, half-lidded and soft with contentment.

It's Matthias who first unspools himself from them, and he balances himself on his elbow and brushes the hair from their faces. His voice, with its deep timbre, is so quiet that she can barely hear it over the fire, despite it diminishing since they first arrived in the room.

"If you still want the gift, you have to drink from me. Do you want it tonight? It doesn't have to be tonight, or ever."

Revenge.

Eternity.

Freedom.

Her neck pulses, and she only wants more. She can still taste the coppery flavor of Léon's blood, can see the dark smear of their mingling blood on Matthias' lips.

She and Léon say at once, embracing one another, "Yes."

Matthias slinks out of bed, and when she raises herself up, her chin burrowed against the uninjured side of Léon's neck, she catches an impressive view of his entire back as he goes to grab a fire poker and stab at the logs, working to stoke the flames.

When he's done, he puts the poker back and saunters to the side of the bed to open the nightstand. He picks something up, and it gleams—a particularly sharp letter opener. When Léon moves on his back to look at Matthias, too, she's reminded of a time when they visited a museum once, when they had enough money to spare, and they both stared at the same painting, leaning into one another, and she marveled at them viewing the same art and history together.

She and Léon unfurl to face Matthias on their knees as he joins them in the rumpled center of the bed, and with one graceful motion, slices open the supple flesh above his heart. And then, he repeats the motion on his other breast, creating two fountains for them to latch on to as, kneeling like supplicants, they press their lips to his leaking chest. Claire eagerly swallows the first tide of blood that hits her tongue, and she basks in the sound of Léon lapping at the blood, too, as she twines her fingers with his.

He looks like he's plunged face-first into a clot of strawberries. She can't help but rub circles into his neck and kiss him, the gesture a loud, messy smack.

"Go on," Claire urges ardently to Matthias, a storm in her heart. "Do it."

A thousand men have tried to kill me with their touches. They beat me and split me open without caring about my name. I was their bitch, their cunt, their trash. And only now will I let it happen with my say.

She and Léon kneel and straighten their backs, and with a look that goes beyond sadness and contemplation, Matthias raises the letter opener.

"Only this once," he whispers, and the horizontal swipe across the air is so swift that she doesn't see it, only tastes the blood welling in her throat—her own—and she hears Léon choke as he falls back. Even though she knows what's happened, she feels bemused and tired, and she rests next to Léon, who still holds her hand, his other clenched around his throat.

Matthias stretches beside Léon.

With a smile, Léon murmurs, "Did…did you know that I dreamed about you?" Claire cannot remember if Léon told her about that, but it's as if he did because she can see the kiss with the moon-fog, the red eyes, as if she were the one who dreamed it.

Matthias' face contorts in pain, and something else soft. "Please don't tell me that. You're going to be all right. Don't hold on to that tether. Just let go."

Léon closes his eyes, his breaths fast and shallow as the blood from the slash at his neck forms a cruel garnet choker. As his life—her life—drains like rain from his body.

She murmurs sleepily, "Your kiss is my grave." And why not? If she has to die, why can't it be a kiss? There are worse ways to go. Alone. Forgotten.

Matthias cups her cheek and presses his bloody lips to his forehead, a seal. "My dear, it's only another life. I hope that soon, a kiss can be something else for you." He continues to coax both of them, his thumb leaving a streak of blood on her cheekbone.

Groggily, she mutters, "I..."

I'm scared. I'm not strong enough. It's been so long since I've prayed. I don't even know if I believe in God more than I believe in Hell.

Despite her assertiveness, she can't help that small pulse of fear; she doesn't know Matthias like Léon does.

Matthias says with a hint of roughness, "If all else fails, I'd storm the gates of the underworld and find both of you."

That makes her dying heart twinge.

She's felt self-reliant for so long. It's good to be watched over and held. And, and...

Let go.

A part of her fights, like it has all her life. She squeezes Léon's hand, the pulse against her thumb weak. The edges of her vision blacken, her attention flowing to the fireside, the easy crackle of flames, and Matthias settles behind Léon and gathers them into his firm, comforting embrace.

Chapter 16

Léon

When they both come back to life again, it's as if they never died, except that they're in a different bedroom near-identical to the one they were in before. Matthias is there, coaxing his palm along their brows and murmuring soft assurances.

After he and Claire wake up, the true Awakening, they spend days cuddling together and half-dozing in Matthias' bed. Léon might've felt a little guilty over sprawling in the bed with his poppy robe—oh, who is he kidding? no, he wouldn't—but the man *did* kill them. It's a fair trade, waking up in that tangle of limbs. He remembers how he once saved a litter of kittens who were huddling outside in the cold, and this is how he feels, like he's burrowing into Claire and Matthias to keep a hold on life.

Or unlife, rather.

Sometimes, he and Claire will be huddled together in the center of the bed, pale and thirsty, while Matthias rests on the end closest to the hearth, stretched out with a book balanced on his chest. He tends to either be in a partially unbuttoned white shirt or completely shirtless.

Other times, needing their sire's proximity, Léon and Claire surround Matthias on both sides and nuzzle their noses and chins against his shoulders, lacing their arms with Matthias'. Léon often wakes up with a fountain of near-sterling hair in his face, mingling with his own in silver-gold streams. The bed suddenly doesn't seem impossibly large.

One late evening, as Matthias lounges and reads *Les Fleurs du mal*, Claire raises her head and mutters hoarsely, "We need blood."

Matthias looks weary, but a soft smile crosses his once-severe and impenetrable features. "Again?" There's some humor Léon wouldn't appreciate if he wasn't ready to bury his teeth in the sinew of the man's throat.

Léon rasps, "If I don't drink, I'll die." He pouts and widens his eyes innocently.

"I'm happy to see your drama made it through the veil of death."

"Fuck you."

"Now, now, my princeling, you need to be good, at least for a minute."

Princeling. Léon has never thought he'd be anyone's prince, but it's a nice thought. He can't help but preen when Matthias pulls his white, lacy shirt over his head, and he retrieves the letter opener to cut those same planes of skin, which has long healed smoothly.

Claire and Léon nestle against Matthias' bleeding chest and lick and suckle. The blood sings more than it did when he was mortal; it burns like whiskey and sends vibrations from his mouth to his groin.

Matthias' life—the shared life of those he's fed on, them (*us*)—freely flows in crimson rivulets. In this moment, Léon can truly feel the ouroboros Matthias speaks about.

They lap and suck at the cuts on his upper chest, curling and rocking against them as they feed.

"Careful," Matthias whispers tenderly to them, voice lined with rare humor. "I think you two are ravenous enough to drain me. It's not usual for someone to have two fledglings at once."

Petulantly, Léon pulls away from the weeping wound briefly, as it's already started to heal around the edges. "Your fault." And then he keeps drinking, licking the dribble of blood before burrowing messily into Matthias' split skin, biting to reopen the cut.

Matthias sets his broad hand on Léon's head and brushes away his tangles. "Yes, my fault, my dear." He cradles Claire's cheek in his other hand, and she leans into his palm and hums in contentment. Her cheeks are regaining color as his blood pulses inside them. As sluggish as he is after death, Léon thinks that he's never felt more alive.

Once they are done, and the fountains dry, he and Claire doze, easy as cats.

He wakes up again between Matthias and Claire, Matthias' back flush against his, Claire's brow on his collarbone.

When he pats his hair, it feels fuller, even if he can't see it in any mirrors. He does know that he'll miss that; without being able to see himself, he's not sure how to perceive himself in any way but through another's eyes.

Ducking his head, he nuzzles himself against Claire's neck.

Stirring, Claire whispers, "I think I have an idea of who I want to drink."

Matthias had insisted that they don't leave so early to confront their harassers, but in the end, he let them go. Shortly before midnight, it doesn't take long until they are back in their apartment for the men to arrive. About five hours of pacing in front of the windows, ensuring that anyone who wants them knows they are there.

There are four men who come, slamming the door open so hard it rattles against the wall, almost falling off its hinges. The men are large and dressed in black, and at the forefront is the man who assaulted them. The brother, unworthy of a remembered name. Gage? Gaston?

He looms over them where they sit on the sofa, and he sneers when, with one violent motion, he crushes a meaty hand under Claire's chin and jerks her to her feet, and two of the other men drag Léon to his feet.

Fury floods through him, and it takes all his strength not to rip out all the bastards' throats. But Claire asked him to wait.

The brother snarls. "For what you did to him, I should fuck both you and your pretty husband bloody."

Claire's bottom lip quivers as she feigns a struggle. "Oh no, *please* stop. I'll do anything you want."

Know when to pull back.

Well.

"*To Hell with that,*" Claire mutters, and only he hears her; he's not even sure if she truly said it aloud, since he never sees her lips move as she goes as if to kiss her captor's throat.

She opens her mouth and sinks her teeth deep into his neck. It isn't the gentle embrace Matthias did in the wine cellar; the man chokes and gurgles, and before his friends can react, she wrenches her head back, a dark, wet shroud of flesh and muscles caught between her teeth as the man releases his grip and bleeds in thick arterial spurts.

Léon leaps on the nearest man, and the whole affair is really quite awkward at first, since he's still not yet convinced himself he can kill again; before, it was a team effort, both at the brothel with the women he befriended and during the two wars.

They grapple clumsily, and something digs in Léon's abdomen—a knife, oh, how *original*, and that's annoying enough that he sinks his teeth in the bobbing column of the man's throat, scratchy and unshaven.

He thought it'd be hard to kill someone, but once he digs into that hot slosh of shredded flesh and blood and torn muscle strings, his mind hazes with needneedneed, and he thinks, *I know why someone would forget their humanity and go mad.* It's that thought alone, when there's a dead body under him and a shock of a bullet in his back, that keeps him from losing himself, aware that *himself* is something that can be taken away.

They rip into the men and gorge themselves before they even have a chance to escape, and kneeling amid the gore, shoveling the blood into his mouth with both hands, Léon feels the bloat of gallons of blood flooding his limbs as he's drenched in it.

Claire stands over the cooling body of the man who assaulted her, and she releases a scream unlike any sound he's heard from her or any living thing. Raw. It pierces through his heart. The closest he's heard was when he and the other whores escaped the brothel and burned the building, leaving the three owners, their cruel pimps, to die. He'd tripped in a rain-soaked cobblestoned alley and had howled with laughter.

Kicking his corpse, Claire screams, *"How does that feel, baby? Does that feel good? You bitch, you whore!"* She kneels down again once, to skewer his gaping chest cavity with her fist.

She's already eaten his heart, he realizes in horror and admiration.

He stops and looks at her as she pants raggedly and stands, teeth set in a wolfish snarl, eyes gleaming unnaturally bright, twin green flames in the night.

Around and below them comes the bustle of footsteps and worried shouts and cries; no one has bust down the door, but they must've heard the screams.

Someone is shouting for a constable, but no one comes. Naturally, they ignored the break-in; none of their business, who cares what happens to two whores? He wonders if he and Claire were the ones screaming, if anyone would've called for the constable before morning.

Instead of worrying, Léon stands and goes over to Claire, and in the heat of what they've done, she cups his jaw, and they crush their lips together in a ruddy smear, a thread of blood between them when they briefly part, only to kiss again and crumple to the floor. They paw and claw and one another, his hand molding against the cleft of her between her legs.

Then, Claire shakes and begins to cry, her tears pinkened with blood.

Stopping and helping her to sit, Léon reaches out and wraps his arms around her. "Oh, my heart." Claire buries her head against his shoulder. They stay like that, frozen except for the occasional shudder of sobs.

It's only when hears the door open that he looks up.

Matthias' look is ashen, but not shocked at the carnage. "Come, we must make haste before the authorities arrive."

Claire

When Claire sinks her teeth into Gabriel's neck, her entire mouth sings, and she shudders in ecstasy as his life flows into her, strengthening her heart as she feels his pulse weaken. Truly, after all those years when he'd beat and fuck her, sometimes in his brother's company, all those years he took her spirit, and she gets to take and take from him, and he can't do anything about it.

When she tears out his heart and bites into it, his blood runs all over her, inside her.

Over him, above all of them, she howls, and the noise rips out of her in a way that might've scraped her throat raw if she were still mortal.

She loves watching him die; after all, he watched her die countless times.

She needs to do something to free the beast clawing at her ribs, as she kisses Léon's and hopes that he might eat her, fuck her.

But it's all too much.

She cries for the girl she used to be, the one who should've been protected and loved, the one who can never have her innocence and girlhood given back.

Claire feels like a child caught being naughty as she and Léon kneel nude on the checkered washroom tiles, as Matthias fills the obscenely large tub with rose-scented water.

She can't find it in herself to speak, filled with every emotion, except one. Affection. Grief. Relief. Happiness. Anger.

But not regret.

Fastidiously, Matthias looks down at them. "You don't need to rest on the floor."

Léon frowns, gazing at the plush of the vanity seat. "We'll ruin the upholstery."

Matthias scoffs. "If you're so worried about that, go ahead and get in the bath."

She stands and looks at the mirror. No one stares back.

It's empty.

They do, and to her surprise, Matthias undresses and joins them.

He douses a legion of washcloths in hot waters and scrubs at their faces and necks; he roves expert, soapy hands over their shoulders.

Claire lets herself be cleaned, as he tenderly rubs the heat into her cheek. And then he wets their hair, and she enjoys it when he massages his fingers into her scalp. Never before had she thought he could be this domestic. It's a quiet and sweet moment, barring the hills of red-soaked washcloths strewn on the porcelain and tiles like cadavers.

Léon asks Matthias, once most of the cleaning is done, "Did you know we'd fail to restrain ourselves, that we'd give into being monsters?"

"I didn't. Being a sire means I must let you make your own choices, even as I guide you. You aren't monsters. You're hurt, and these are your wounds. I will try, in time, to help you heal them, even if it takes centuries. Even if I'm still learning to recognize my own."

Léon replies, looking over at her with concern, "We have nothing but time."

Chapter 17

Léon

"Have you read every single book in here?" Léon asks, surveying the ceiling-high bookshelves lining one hall of the dark study.

Sitting at a mahogany writing desk by the fire, Matthias says, leaning an elbow against the wood, "No. I find it a little sad, the idea of completing them all and having nothing else to read."

Léon shrugs, still standing at the door. "There are always new books being written."

He must look troubled because Matthias looks at him and asks, "What's on your mind?"

"She needed to do it."

Gravely, Matthias replies, "I know." He stands and moves to the burgundy sofa by the fire, motioning for Léon to sit beside him; he does. "It's normal to be...stunned after doing something like that. Did you ever kill anyone in your wars?"

Léon nods. Is Matthias trying to comfort him? Let him know Claire will be okay?

"And you?" Matthias catches a curl and tucks it behind Leon's ear, which now feels a little more like Matthias'. "Did you need to do it?"

"Yes."

A lump forms in his throat as Matthias takes his hand in his. Any other time, and he would've relished this simple intimacy. But...

He *doesn't* entirely know that Matthias won't abandon them like everyone else, and that thought terrifies and shames him. There's no reason for him to distrust Matthias, but every part of him tells him that he can't ever fully trust anyone even when he tells his idiot mind to calm down and let himself be content.

His idiot mind.

When he looks into Matthias' eyes, something cracks in him, brittle as thin glass. The first sob escapes, and Matthias reaches his other hand to clasp the crown of Léon's head, gently guiding him to his chest, where Léon cries.

Claire

In their bed, formerly known as Matthias', Léon kneads his knuckles into her back. "Beloved, how are you feeling?" They're alone for now; often at night, Matthias will knit or read in his study. Sometimes, Léon joins him at Claire's encouragement, but she knows he's worried about her, which makes her feel guilty.

She searches her mind for the absolute truth because she's not sure even she knows. She isn't sad about killing Gabriel, but there's a mourning for what it might mean for her, her soul, like Matthias said.

"I know that one day I will feel better. I need to exist as this for now."

Léon leans his forehead against her temple. "That's okay. I'll be here with you, also existing. As long as it takes, eternally."

They embrace.

"Léon," murmurs Claire, "do I frighten you?"

"No. *Never*. I'm happy for you. Happy for us. I'm happy to have such strong companions. I wouldn't have you any other way. And don't forget, I was right there with you."

At dusk, the three of them sit in the garden among fireflies at a small, white circular table. Claire admires a trellis of roses and a light layer of deep green moss on the side of the stone home. She roves a finger over the tight three strings of pearls, smooth as eyes, around her throat.

She looks down at her teacup before she raises it. "How on earth do you keep this from congealing?"

Matthias straightens in his chair, a rare, adorable gleam in his eyes because he gets to explain something science-related. "An experiment I've done on crushed maidenhair leaves."

"You'll have to tell me more about your chemistry one day."

After a brief lull, stirring his spoon in his blood-tea, Léon asks Matthias, "Will we need coffins?"

"Yes, I thought we could try to have you two practice sleeping in them. You'll feel more rejuvenated in them."

Léon raises a brow. "Why is that?"

"It's the best way to be in absolute darkness and solitude. Or, if you two want, you can sleep in my coffin for a few nights until you adjust."

Léon smirks. "You have a coffin that fits three people?"

Matthias haughtily lifts his nose, which Léon flicks. "I like my space."

Claire claps her hands together. "Can we pick ours out?" It's morbidly exciting to think about having a pretty coffin.

"Yes," Matthias says softly. The two men almost look relieved when she enters the conversation with some measure of cheer.

This life will be worth it, she knows it will. They'll make it so. Perhaps her only regret is that she has no women as companions any longer. It isn't that Léon and Matthias aren't enough, or that them being men detracts from their company; it's just that she relates to them in a different way than she's related to other women like her in the past. She can't quite explain it.

There's still a part of her that feels singular, disconnected. She hopes it doesn't linger.

"Where would you like to go?" Matthias asks them. "The human world is endless."

Claire looks down at her cup. "We're human, aren't we?"

Matthias hums and rubs his chin. "Yes, I suppose we are."

Claire says breathlessly, "Despite everything, I've always wanted to see America. It's just so vast. And new." She's known many women who've run off to America for a new start.

"I do have some properties there."

"Some?" Léon inquires, leaning in his chair and crossing one leg over the other. "How many, exactly?"

"Three. As you said, it's a very vast country. However, it's not as forward-thinking there as it is here."

Claire says, hands in her lap, "Perhaps not now, but who knows what'll happen in the next decade, or the next century. Here, there. And we can always come back if we wish. After enough time."

Matthias meets her eyes intensely. "Where exactly in America would we go?"

"I'm amenable to anything. I do have a lovely property in Massachusetts, above a small hollow near the ocean."

Léon asks, "And close to a misty cemetery?"

Matthias gives a small shrug. "I can't help that the property was less expensive near a graveyard. And it was rather old, too."

Claire mutters, "I suppose the ship rats won't sustain us."

"It will be a hard journey, but not impossible if you sleep throughout. You mustn't leave your coffin."

Léon replies, "All right. I think I can do that. You know I do my best when I must be completely still and silent."

"Right," Matthias says.

Pacing by the bed, Léon pokes at the pointed top of his ear. "Now, this will take some getting used to."

Lounging on a chaise at the end of the bed, Claire says, "I think these make us look rather ethereal."

With a huff, Léon extends both his arms from his sides and flops into bed backwards.

Rising, Claire starts, "Léon, I—is that a cravat?"

Léon strokes the ruffles, still on his back. "What? I think it looks rather dashing on me."

Claire smiles, fully standing. "Perhaps I should wear one, too."

"You should. Trust me, there are plenty to go around. If Matthias ever ran out of any other clothes, he could still traipse around with nothing but those around his neck."

"You'd like that."

Raising his head, Léon grins. His eyes shine. "Maybe."

"You two could always knit some new clothes together." She remembers how she cried when Léon made her two dark green gloves when she complained about her hands growing numb with cold in the winter.

"Yes," Léon murmurs, and she joins him. They rest in bed, but it doesn't feel entirely right until Matthias comes in.

Léon

Matthias is right: Even with a cap on, the sun horribly fatigues him. Claire's bonnet only augments the shadows under her eyes. Léon presses a kiss to her knuckles as the wind sways her immaculate velvet wine-red gown with back sequin-roses beneath her fur coat, and it ruffles his hair as the waves whisper and a ship horn bellows among the caterwauls of seagulls. The world is dark behind his round sunglasses.

"You know," Léon says to Matthias, who wears a large black, cloth duster that reaches past his knees. "I didn't think we could cross running water."

"That," Matthias says, taking his hand in the shade of the buildings above the harbor, "would be inconvenient."

Claire steps forward, her suede pumps making the bridge planks creak as she looks at the horizon through the dark shades. A wash of cigar smoke and chatter and sea salt washes over them. An entire sprawling world, open to them.

"A new life," she says wistfully.

Léon and Matthias look at each other, lost in each other's eyes.

Yes, at last.

About the Author

Morgan is a horror, fantasy, and romance author. They have a soft spot for all things dark and gothic, especially vampires and an array of castle-dwelling monsters. They've also never written an angel that they didn't want to make a little weird-looking, at least. They live in the Southern United States with a menagerie of ill-behaved cats and dogs, including a malevolent tortoiseshell named Satan. More about their work can be found at morgandante.com. Baby bat and possum photos can be found on Twitter at @morgansinferno.

Milton Keynes UK
Ingram Content Group UK Ltd.
UKHW021348050424
440689UK00007B/195